Christmas Stalking

By Selena Kitt

eXcessica publishing

Christmas Stalking © 2017 by Selena Kitt

Excessica LLC
486 S. Ripley #164
Alpena MI 49707

To order additional copies of this book, contact:
books@excessica.com
www.excessica.com

Cover design © 2017 Willsin Rowe
First Edition: 2008
Second Edition (Home for Christmas – Emme Rollins): December 2014
Third Edition: December 2017

Chapter One

A police siren howled in the early morning haze. Ginny woke with a start, stifling a scream and cowering in the cold, dark vestibule. She drew a shaky breath, the images of her dream lingering. She found it difficult to differentiate between memory and imagination—everything felt like a threat. Pulling her coat around her, she sought warmth and comfort and found neither. Instead, her mind flooded with the memory of his bruising grip, the push and pull that inevitably led to more pain.

This was the only place she felt even remotely safe. She didn't know how they stayed in business anymore—everyone downloaded their movies and people who did still rent them never returned movies after midnight. It was a gamble but, so far, her assessment had been accurate. The local family video store's little cubbyhole was dark and, though it wasn't heated, it was at least twenty degrees warmer than outside. Best of all, it was great protection from the wind.

It was the perfect place to curl up and sleep, tucked into the corner of the vestibule between the two doors. The glassed-in area served as the perfect nook, a six by six square of relative warmth and safety. The store couldn't lock the outer door because, to return movies, customers had to access the flip-top slot located inside the little foyer. Luckily for Ginny, the "Return Movies Here" bin never saw any action until people were on their way to work in the morning, and by then, she was already up and looking for breakfast.

If it were a big chain store like Blockbuster used to be, she would've been worried about security cameras or even guards patrolling. This, though, was just a little mom-and-pop operation, a family video store where the kids' movies were always free and they gave away popcorn with every rental—anything to try and stay in business. In a small town like this, there were still plenty of people who couldn't afford to trade in their VHS collection for DVDs, let alone Blu-rays.

She always set her watch alarm and forced herself to make it out the door while it was still dark and she could slip behind the strip mall unnoticed. The world was a different place at five in the morning. It was something she had never known on those school days before her older sister, Maggie, had left them. After that, it was just Ginny and their stepfather, Brody, alone together in a very small space.

The morning was still and empty. Each eerily haloed streetlight became both a beacon and an announcement. She found herself stepping around the orange-tinged circles, as if crossing that barrier would set off an ominous warning, some universal alarm.

She discovered a veritable smorgasbord behind the strip mall, where there was a Chinese carryout restaurant and a Dunkin' Donuts. Donut holes were prone to going stale and she could often find enough of those to stave off the gnawing hole in her belly. She'd been afraid to eat the leftovers from the Chinese restaurant, but had found little stapled wax paper packages of egg rolls on several occasions that had been a real treat.

Then she discovered the houses behind the alleyway. Most of them put their trash out on Tuesdays, and she had found a myriad of treasures—a pair of gloves with a hole in one thumb, several mismatched pairs of socks, and some old, scratched up Matchbox cars for her nephews. She'd been fortunate at the house behind the alleyway of the video store, and she wasn't disappointed this morning. In a box next to the trash was a lucky find—an unopened jar of Jif peanut butter, a small bottle of apple juice and a Scrunchie ponytail holder. Her stomach lurched at the sight of peanut butter!

She shoved the bottle of apple juice in her coat pocket and slipped the Scrunchie over her wrist. She unscrewed the lid of the peanut butter and peeled back the foil, breaking the creamy, smooth surface with her index finger. She licked it off, sucking hard to get it all. Pure peanuty heaven! Her stomach growled and she satisfied it as fast as she could without a spoon, fingering as much as she could into her mouth at a time. It was like buttery velvet melting on her tongue. She wasn't even aware she was making little mewling noises, like a starving kitten settling in to nurse, or that she had wandered under the light of a streetlamp.

That's when she saw him out of the corner of her eye, standing less than ten feet away to her right. She took an immediate step back, thinking fast enough to put the lid back on her peanut butter and slip it into her other coat pocket. Beyond him was the shortest route to open space and freedom. Behind her was a very long alleyway that didn't break out into a clearing for the length of a football field.

She couldn't make out his features in the shadows, just that he was big, very big, even taller than her stepfather and wider across the shoulders by far. He looked like he had run the length of several football fields in his time, and she guessed he could run down the stretch of the alleyway after her without breaking a sweat.

Ginny took a step back, then another, her instincts moving her of their own volition. He didn't move toward her, just stood there in the darkness, watching. That's when she noticed the white plastic bag he was holding by his left side. Her heart hammered faster as she realized he must live in the house where she rummaged almost daily through the trash can. He was just taking out the garbage.

She tried to think of something to say, maybe apologize, explain, but instead she turned and ran. The pavement was slippery—last night's sleet had left a sheet of ice over the blacktop. She didn't care, she just ran, skidding once into the dumpster behind Dunkin' Donuts, where she would've normally stopped to look for confections. She didn't dare look back. She thought she heard him call out to her, "Hey! Come back!" but she wasn't sure. It might have been her imagination or just her heart pounding in her ears.

She wondered how she could even dare to go back to her spot at the video store. Lamenting the possible loss of her hiding place, Ginny shoved her hands into her pockets, put her head down against the wind, and began to walk the three blocks to the 7-Eleven. The convenience store clerk was a young kid who worked there on weekdays. He watched her walk to the back to use the bathroom like she did every other morning. This bathroom was perfect, very clean, one toilet, a sink and a door that locked behind her. The one she used at the Shell station across the street wasn't as nice and didn't have the hand dryer, which she had found invaluable.

Ginny shrugged her backpack off and peeled back layers of clothing. Her long heavy jacket, wool outside and padded inside, was blessedly warm. It had been her mother's. It was followed by a sweater, a turtleneck, a sports bra, heavy hiking boots, a pair of jeans over two pairs of leggings and two pairs of socks.

She stood in front of the cracked mirror, shivering in her panties, and turned on the water to let it get warm while she rummaged in her backpack for the case that held her soap, toothbrush and toothpaste.

Something small and square fell out of the bag and clattered against the tile. She gasped, snatching it back up and holding it close to her chest. It seemed impossible something so small could be her only hope of safety. The memory card was no bigger than a stamp. It had once been in a camcorder and it bore no label, nothing to reveal the horror it contained. She tucked it back into her bag, burying it deep, like a treasure, then turned her attention back to her morning routine.

Sometimes, she could hear people in the store, customers or the clerk, talking to one another, but no one had ever come knocking on the door during her morning ritual. Her panties came off, and she peed, her bladder near bursting, then she washed her panties in the sink using her ever-dwindling bar of soap. She was going to have to figure out how to get another. Both bathrooms only had the liquid kind.

It was a lesson in acrobatics trying to wash at the sink. Leaning over, she washed her face, then her white-blonde hair, which she did every other day, but never on days when it was below freezing. She scrubbed her upper body, her ribs prominent, belly concave. She managed to clean the light blonde thatch of pubic hair by straddling the sink, scooping water with her hands to rinse.

After drying off with paper towels, she wrung out the water from her hair as well as she could, and then bent over in front of the hand dryer in an attempt to dry her hair. She brushed her teeth, sad to lose the taste of peanut butter in her mouth, but smiling at the thought of the rest of the jar in her pocket. She used the newly found Scrunchie to pull her hair back. That was her second favorite find this morning, something she hadn't thought to throw in her backpack when she left. She was going to really appreciate it on her daily walks, when the wind whipped her long hair against her face so hard it made her gasp.

When her hair was mostly dry, it was time to get re-dressed. She put on a clean pair of underwear and did a quick smell-test on the clothing closest to her body—leggings, turtleneck, socks. Then, she began the process of pulling it all on again, layer after layer. She struggled to zip up her jeans over the two pairs of leggings, and put her foot up on the toilet lid so she could lace her hiking boots.

Dressed and warm again, she dried the washed panties under the dryer and stuffed them into her backpack. She tried to take a less obvious way out of the store, edging along the dairy cooler and past the magazine rack. She didn't know if they cared if she used the bathroom, or even if they noticed, but she didn't want to find out.

It was already warming up outside, although her watch said it was only 6:15 a. m. She'd been lucky so far. Michigan winters could be brutal, but they were also unpredictable. It could be forty degrees in December, like it felt today might be, or it could be close to zero—below that with the wind chill. She didn't know how well the video store was going to protect her from the elements at night if they started hitting the single digits. She was going to have to scout out some other possibilities, and soon, but not today. It would take her an hour to walk to the shelter to see Maggie. She had promised to visit on Tuesday and she hated disappointing her nephews.

Thankfully, the boys were waiting for her when she arrived, because she dreaded going into the shelter. She kept praying the women's shelter's claims to Maggie were true—that they were invisible, anonymous, unable to be found, even by law enforcement—not only for Maggie and the boys' sakes, but her own as well. If Brody managed to find them, she was dead.

Her chest constricted, remembering The Mission Shelter in downtown Millsberg, her little hometown. She'd been there in the soup line, something to ease the ache in her belly, but she'd looked up and seen Brody, a paragon of virtue and civic duty, doling out food to the less fortunate.

She'd thought she could slip out unnoticed, but he'd seen her, his eyes darkening, mouth twisting into a fast snarl as he pursued her through the kitchen and past the dumpsters. She knew he sometimes volunteered, but had this been a coincidence or was he looking for her? She lost him at the last moment, ducking into an unlocked warehouse and huddling in the bathroom until dark. In that moment, she realized how much danger she was really in, that just her presence meant serious trouble for Maggie and the boys.

Even all the way over here in Lewisonville.

"Aunt Ginny! Let's go, let's go, let's go!" The boys chanted, jumping around her like they were on pogo sticks. She laughed and, putting one hand on Sean's mop of red hair and the other on Michael's fine blonde curls, she turned them back toward the building.

"Go get your mom," she instructed. "You guys meet me over there at the park and I'll push you on the swings. Ready? Go!"

They tore off running, coats unzipped and flying out behind them. She watched them jostle for position at the door. Sean looked more like Brody every time she saw him, and his reed-like figure next to Michael's substantial bulk made them look less like brothers than any two boys she'd seen. They had the same stark blue eyes and Maggie's upturned nose, but that was as far as any similarities went.

When they burst out of the door again only a few minutes later, Maggie followed, shrugging off her coat and calling after them to slow down. They hit Ginny from behind with the force of two small whirling tornadoes, knocking the wind out of her. She gasped, picked up Michael, swung him onto her hip and held him there with one hand, while she took Sean's hand with the other. Maggie fell in line next to them, breathless from trying to catch up to the boys.

"I'm on kitchen duty today. Sorry I wasn't out here. I know you hate going in," she apologized, reaching to tug a twig out of Sean's hood.

Ginny shrugged, whispering nonsense into Michael's ear and making him giggle and pull away.

"I didn't have to go in. The monster patrol was out here waiting for me, weren't ya?" Ginny tousled Sean's irresistible mop again. He ducked and rolled his eyes, sticking out his tongue at her.

"They were? Sean and Michael, I told you to stay inside those doors, didn't I?" Maggie admonished.

The boys pretended they hadn't heard her, Michael wiggling to get down when Sean challenged, "Let's race to the swings!" and off they went.

"I'll be glad to start that temp job next week." Maggie tucked her hands into her coat pockets. "They need more structure than this place. They'll have preschool in the morning and the shelter helped me find daycare for the afternoons. Now if we could only find our own place..."

"What happened to that little apartment on Fourth Street?"

They sat on the park bench, watching the boys struggle to get their bottoms onto the big-boy swings, their legs dangling uselessly. Ginny knew it was only moments before they were going to call out to her, "Swing me, swing me, do underdog!" She waited, wanting to hear what her sister had to say.

"Oh, Gin, it's so perfect!" Maggie clutched Ginny's arm in excitement. "A bedroom a piece for the boys! But the landlord wants the first month's rent and a security deposit—that's a thousand dollars! Do you know how long it's going to be before I can save that kind of money?"

Maggie's eyes, shining just moments ago, now welled up with tears. "I thought we'd be out of here by Christmas. I don't want them to have to spend Christmas in a shelter."

"I know." Ginny's jaw tightened. She looked back out toward the swings where Sean had generously gotten down to give his brother a start-push.

"How are things at home now?" Maggie attempted a change of subject, wiping guiltily at her eyes. "Brody isn't bothering you, is he?"

"It's fine," Ginny lied. "He was never like that with me, Maggie. It was bad for a couple of days after I went back, and of course he wanted to know where I was for those two days, and I wouldn't tell him I was at your place, or where you were."

"I'm so sorry, Gin. If I'd known..." Maggie apologized for the three hundredth time. "Tim took everything, just everything. I didn't have a choice but to come here."

"Listen, it's just my luck, right?" Ginny waved it away. "I try to run away from home, then my sister's crackhead husband sells everything she owns and she gets evicted and I have nowhere else to go. What else is new? How is this any different than anything in my life?"

Ginny's laugh was grim, and Maggie placed her hand on her sister's arm.

"I know. I pick real winners, don't I?" Maggie snorted. "And you know, we had such a great role model growing up..."

That particular irony forced Ginny's wry smile. Brody was the only father either of them had known.

"When I get a place, you can come live with me, okay?" Maggie assured her.

"I think I'm going to head out to somewhere warm—California or Florida." Ginny's eyes turned to the horizon. "Find some surfer guy and be a beach bunny. What do you think?"

"I think it would be a waste."

Ginny had spent many of her days tucked away in a warm corner of the library. During her Internet searches, she had found a support network, a sort of Underground Railroad for victims of domestic violence that would help her escape Brody's long reach. It was an entire network that could hide her, even provide her with a new identity, if she wanted one. California was as far away as she could imagine. It meant a cross-country trip, but she would finally be free.

She just wished Maggie and the boys would come with her. But she knew better. Her sister was hardly the adventurous type, and although Maggie denied it, Ginny knew she wasn't over Tim. Some part of Maggie was still hoping they'd get back together, as sick as that horrible idea was. Ginny knew it even before her sister pressed the safe deposit key into her hand and asked her to empty the contents—if there was anything left.

"I put you on my account, remember?" Maggie reminded her, with such hope in her eyes. "I don't think Tim would have remembered the safety deposit box. Do you?"

Ginny thought Tim would have remembered to check the sofa cushions for change to feed his habit, but she didn't say that. Instead, she took the key and said she'd check the box for her sister. Except the box was at a bank in their little home town, two hours away. Maggie thought Ginny was still there, living with Brody, not sleeping on the streets, too afraid to go home.

Ginny knew she could lie and tell Maggie there was nothing left in the box, and the odds were, she'd be right. But what if the thousand dollars Maggie had socked away was really still in there? That would pay for the little apartment her sister wanted to rent. And it would serve Tim right, if he really had forgotten about it. Heck, even Maggie had forgotten about it, until she was cleaning out her purse and found the key.

There was so much hope in her sister's eyes, she just couldn't say no. Besides, she had no reason to, at least as far as Maggie knew. And she couldn't tell Maggie the truth. Not now, not ever. The problem was, Ginny didn't have the money for a bus ticket, so she would have to hitchhike her way back to their little hometown.

It was a bad idea, she knew. A very, very bad idea. Not necessarily the hitchhiking—although that probably wasn't smart either—but the place she grew up was even smaller than the town Maggie and the boys were sheltered in now. It was a place she might be noticed, and it was a very great risk.

"Come on, let's go play on the swings." Ginny stood, relenting to the demanding calls coming their way as she pocketed the key.

Maggie grabbed her hand as they walked, squeezing gently. Ginny fought hot, bitter tears and lost, letting the wind dry them as she ran under Michael's swing again and again and again.

Chapter Two

Barnes and Noble was the perfect place to spend a quiet afternoon sketching. Normally, she would be drawing figures—people browsing books or sitting and drinking coffee in the café. But she was working on something for the boys she needed to finish before Christmas. The clerk, Robbie, set another tea down for her and she smiled at him gratefully. She wasn't paying for the treats he left on her table and he was risking a great deal doing it. In the past, he'd even slipped sketch pads and pencils into her bag for her to find later.

"How's it coming?" He slid into the chair beside her. She turned her pad to show him a fair likeness of Wolverine.

"Wow," he breathed, sounding truly impressed. "Are you sure you want to waste that as a coloring book for a four-year-old?"

She just smiled, continuing to sketch, looking now and then at the book in front of her, *X-Men Legends Volume III*, which she'd pulled earlier from the shelves. She would put it back before she left.

"Break?" She glanced at the counter where a few people drank lattes, reading a newspaper or paperback.

"Yep, only five more hours and I'm off for the day," he groaned. "Want to come home with me for a Hungry Man dinner?"

She lifted her eyes to him, seriously tempted. A TV dinner sounded fantastic. The two almond cookies he'd slipped her were just enough to make her stomach remember food. It came down to not knowing him well enough to trust walking into a man's place alone, even if he was nice to her. Besides, she knew what he was ultimately interested in, and she intended to keep him firmly in the "friend-zone."

"That's the guy who was in here the other day watching you." Robbie's voice lowered, giving her a reprieve from answering his question.

Ginny's breath caught, and she looked up, locating the man over by the philosophy section. Her worries about trusting Robbie suddenly paled in comparison as she stared at the man the clerk pointed out. He was half-turned away from them now, and she recognized him immediately—his bulk, the way his broad shoulders stretched the fabric of his dark blue winter jacket, the sureness of his chin.

She'd seen him yesterday outside the Shell station, and the day before that, he was at the library where she was looking up comic book characters. Her nagging suspicion that he was a private detective, someone sent by Brody to follow her, was growing. She started gathering up her things, shoving her sketchbook into her bag.

"Hey, where are you going?" Robbie questioned. "It's only one o'clock."

"I know. Can you put this back for me?" She slid the X-Men book across the table toward him. He nodded, watching her pull on her coat and backpack. "I'll probably see you tomorrow."

"Probably?"

She shrugged, jerking her head toward the man who had moved down the aisle toward them, into what she assumed was closer listening distance. She edged her way around the café, walking the furthest perimeter she could, and slipped down a darkened corridor and into the women's bathroom, relieved to find it empty.

She went into a stall and struggled to pull all her layers down so she could pee. Her hands shook as she washed them at the sink and she took a few deep breaths, trying to slow her racing heart. She took her ponytail out, smoothed her hair with her hands, peering at her face, noting the beginnings of dark circles under her eyes. Five hours of sleep a night was beginning to take its toll.

Ginny rubbed her hands together under the dryer, telling herself she was trembling because of the temperature in the restroom. She struggled to keep her mind off the man on the other side of the wall—and off the man she was sure had hired him to find her.

Brody had probably just called in a favor. Private detectives were almost always ex-cops and she could see Brody calling some buddy who used to be on the force, faking concern about his missing stepdaughter. *"She's wild. I'm worried what she could be into. I just want her home safe."* In reality, for Brody, it would be a simple business transaction, just a matter of retrieving his property. Maggie he considered damaged goods, but Ginny was still valuable to him.

Her nails dug into her palms and she'd bitten her lip so hard it was bleeding. She was safer sleeping on the streets and living out of garbage cans, but no one would believe that. No one ever believed that.

The door opened, and she gasped, whirling around, wide-eyed. A mother with a baby in her arms swept into the bathroom, looking almost as tired as Ginny felt. The woman smiled an apology, taking the baby to the foldout counter to change its diaper.

It was a tiny little baby and Ginny could remember when Maggie had Sean, how small and delicate he had felt in her arms when she first held him. All throughout

Maggie's pregnancy, after she began to show and Brody had kicked her out, Ginny still hadn't understood Maggie's insistence on having and keeping a baby fathered by a man they both despised and feared. She didn't understand it all the way up until she had held Sean in her arms, looked into those guileless eyes, and realized it wasn't the baby's fault.

The image of Brody in her head obliterated all rational thought. Ginny washed her hands again, stalling for time. The young mother cooed and clucked at her baby as she worked, folding over tabs and refastening snaps. Ginny turned on the dryer, standing there as long as she dared, until her hands were so warm they started to turn red. She shouldered her backpack and glanced behind her.

The mother lifted the baby, kissing her. It was a girl, if the pink giraffe on the sleeper was any indication. Ginny wondered for a moment if anyone had ever held and kissed her that way. She doubted it. Maybe Maggie, three years older than her, had loved her that way once, but it was no substitute for a mother.

Ginny pulled open the door, steeling herself to find him just outside, but the corridor was empty. She edged around the corner, watchful, but didn't see him. Robbie was behind the counter at the café, doling out cappuccinos and biscotti.

She walked toward the exit and she was almost to the door when she realized she'd left her Scrunchie on the bathroom counter. She stopped, vacillating, not wanting to leave it there but desperate for escape. Watching the wind whip the bare branches of trees outside and imagining the hour-long trek back toward the video store, she made her decision.

She turned and hurried back toward the women's bathroom. The young mother was gone, but the black Scrunchie was still there. She snatched at it and started putting her hair back up as she headed out of the bathroom.

Both hands were busy behind her head as she came out of the door, and if she hadn't stopped to tighten the band, she never would have seen him standing in a slanted shadow in the corner. It was the white Barnes & Noble bag in his hand that caught her eye. There was a moment of déjà-vu and a flicker of a memory stirred before he spoke.

"I didn't mean to scare you." His voice was low and kind, and it startled her on many levels. Her heartbeat quickened when she met his eyes, and found them strangely kind as well.

She mumbled, "That's okay," tearing her gaze away and edging toward the exit.

He stepped further into the light and she saw his face, sure now he was the same man she'd seen yesterday, and the day before, too. There was something about him that was familiar, but she couldn't quite identify it. He didn't move to touch her or speak again—he just watched her, smiling. She felt like a cornered mouse, sitting between cat's paws.

"Is that yours?" He nodded behind her.

She turned and was horrified to discover her sketchbook lying in front of the bathroom door. She scooped it up, hugging it to her chest.

"Thanks." She moved to sail past him and he touched her arm. It was like a jolt and she couldn't help her gasp.

"Are you an artist?"

As he pried into her life, she felt her fear changing into something else. Her eyes narrowed, her mouth drawing into a small, thin line as she stood and assessed him. He was three times her size at least, but then again, they were in the middle of a bookstore. He wouldn't dare try anything here, would he?

"Why don't you ask your buddy the cop about me? He thinks he knows everything!" Ignoring the feigned, puzzled look on his face, she fled toward the exit, still clinging to her sketchbook.

She had walked fifteen blocks before she remembered it. She stopped to put it away and, this time, she zipped her backpack.

She actually thought about asking Robbie for a ride. She knew he would give her one, but then she'd feel like she owed him something, and that wasn't a good idea. Not that riding next to a portly fifty-year-old hunter wearing camouflage and an orange hat, the kind with the flaps, was a much better one. He kept forgetting her fake name—Sarah—but at least he didn't try to put his hands anywhere on her person. He just talked about his own daughter—*about your age*—and her courses at the local community college.

He chatted the whole way, and that was fine with Ginny. She didn't want to make conversation anyway. She'd been lucky to get picked up soon after sticking out her thumb, only to discover the woman was only going ten miles down the road. This guy—Brad—had picked her up outside a little hole-in-the-wall bar, and she'd been a little afraid to get into his big pick-up at first, but his talk about his daughter had assuaged her fears. A little, anyway.

Now that they were almost to Millsberg, she knew he was harmless. She was heading toward the real danger. Back into town, where Brody lived and worked, where too many people knew her.

"You can let me off at the McDonalds." Ginny pointed to the glowing, golden arches. "My friend is picking me up."

A lie. She had no idea how she was going to get back to Lewisonville. She'd figure something out later. But the McDonalds was next to the PNC Bank, and it was the bank she wanted. It was almost four o'clock and they closed at five.

"Thanks for the ride!" she called, hopping down from the high seat, closing the door on the man's lengthy reply.

Ginny's stomach ached with hunger. Brad had offered her a granola bar, which she had eaten, but it had only managed to activate the grumbling in her belly. The smell of fries and grease was overpowering. It made her knees feel weak as she walked toward the well-lit storefront. Behind her, Brad turned his big truck right out of the lot, heading toward the deer camp where he was hoping to bag a big buck with his bow.

She didn't even like venison—Brody was a hunter, too, and had filled their freezer with the chewy, gamey meat—but she thought she could eat a whole deer right about now, antlers and all. Instead of torturing herself by walking into the McDonalds, she crossed the parking lot, went over the grassy embankment, and into the bank.

It was late on a Friday and the deposit line was long. Ginny glanced around, hoping she didn't see anyone she knew. Her sister had put her on the account last year, and a tall, angular woman with a lot of dark hair and red lipstick had helped them then, but Ginny didn't see her. Maggie and Tim had been separated at the time—one of the many times—and Maggie had dragged Ginny down to the bank to put some "important papers" into the safety deposit box and add her to the account.

Ginny didn't know if Maggie had ever told Tim, but the lady at the bank didn't seem too concerned at the time, since Maggie was on the account and making the request. She just hoped no one would give her a hard time about it today. As long as she didn't run into anyone who knew her...

"Virginia?"

The sound of her full name, someone calling out from behind her, made her wince. Of course. It was probably her nosey neighbor, who would run straight back and tell Brody he'd seen her. Ginny glanced over her shoulder and blinked in surprise at her seventh-grade math teacher. He'd been old back then, but now he looked like he was going on eighty.

"Oh, hi, Mr. Spencer." Ginny smiled, waggling her fingers at him, standing hunched over in line, his pants pulled up practically to his nipples. At least, as far as she knew, Mr. Spencer and Brody didn't run in the same circles.

"Can I help you?" The teller waved Ginny to the window and she told the girl—honestly, she looked no older than Ginny, maybe twenty, with curly red hair—what she wanted, pulling the safety deposit key out of her jeans pocket.

"Let me call the manager," the little redhead said, picking up the phone.

Ginny waited, her heart beating so fast she thought it might just gallop right out of her chest. The manager happened to be the dark-haired woman with the bright red lipstick she remembered from when they opened the account, but the woman didn't seem to remember Ginny. She just looked at Ginny's I.D., had her write her name on a card, and then matched the signatures.

"Okay, come with me." The tall woman's heels—those were red, too—clacked on the tile as she led Ginny away from the lobby. The bank manager used her key to unlock one of the locks on the safety deposit box. "I'll leave you alone for a few minutes."

"Thanks." Ginny gave her the same smile and wave she'd given to Mr. Spencer.

Please let there be a million dollar in here.

Or at least a thousand, she thought. She could use a little of it for bus fare home. And maybe she could afford a Happy Meal to take with her. That would be divine, right about now.

Ginny put the key in and turned it, closing her eyes before pulling open the box like it was Christmas. She got up the courage to open them, peeking first with one eye. Then she opened both of them with a long, deep sigh. No money. Just a bunch of papers. She rifled through them, hoping maybe to find something good— a bond she could cash in, some life insurance with cash value, maybe—but it was just the boys' birth certificates and Maggie and Tim's marriage license. If there had been a thousand dollars in the box at one time, it wasn't there anymore.

"We meet again, Virginia."

She startled, her hand going to her throat, as Mr. Spencer came in, followed by the red-heeled manager woman. Ginny grabbed the papers out and locked up her own box.

"Hi, Mr. Spencer," Ginny said again, clearing her throat and taking a step back. "I'm done here. Thanks."

The bank manager locked up Ginny's box with her key, putting it back. It was empty now. Then she took out another box—Mr. Spencer's, Ginny assumed—and unlocked it with her key.

"Nice seeing you," Ginny said, as she walked past her old—now, very old—math teacher. "Bye now."

"Goodbye, Virginia," he called.

Chapter Three

Ginny stopped in the lobby to shove the papers into her backpack. Mr. Spencer was still in the back, presumably stuffing his safe deposit box full of stock certificates. Or ketchup packets. Either way, it was more than Ginny had. She put her backpack on and braced herself against the wind as she went out into the cold. No money, nowhere to stay even if she found a way back, and she was starving. All she wanted was a warm bed and a cheeseburger. She'd even be happy with one of those sloppy McDonald's cheeseburgers with the fake meat and the crooked cheese.

She stood there looking at those golden arches for a minute, the wind cutting through her like a knife. Maybe if she went inside and sat at a table for a while, someone would forget to throw away their garbage. It wouldn't be the first time she'd been hungry enough to eat someone else's food.

"Would you like to get a cup of coffee, Virginia?"

"Mr. Spencer!" Ginny grabbed at her chest again. It was the third time he'd nearly given her a heart attack.

"Caribou Coffee, right across the street." He nodded toward the bright, cheery coffee house packed with people coming and going, ordering coffee and all sorts of sandwiches and pastries. "I'm buying."

Ginny studied him for a moment, considering, but her stomach decided for her. Besides, how much trouble could she get into with her eighty-year-old former math teacher? The man even took her arm when they crossed the street, for pete's sake.

"So, what have you been up to, Virginia?" Mr. Spencer asked once they'd ordered—coffee for him, black, and a cherry Coke for her, made with real cherry syrup, according to the barista. She also ordered a ham and cheese sandwich and a cherry tart. She felt bad for ordering food on his dime, but he insisted she get what she wanted, and she was hungry. Dizzyingly hungry. "Did you graduate?"

"Last June," she replied through a delicious mouthful of croissant, cheese, and pork. It was the best thing she'd ever tasted. Even the peanut butter in her pocket paled in comparison.

"College then?" he sipped his coffee, tilting his head at her, speculative. "You were always very bright."

"Art school." It was just a little white lie. "In the fall. I'm just... I'm not doing much right now."

"Art school." He pursed his thin lips and nodded like any typical math teacher would. Art school was impractical. Illogical. "Scholarship?"

She just nodded, wolfing down her sandwich. It was almost gone and her stomach, used to far less food, was stretched to capacity, but she kept going anyway. He was watching her with a strange, curious look on his face, like she was an interesting specimen he'd found under a microscope. Which would have been an apt metaphor, if he'd taught science.

"I guess you retired, huh?" she asked, sipping her Coke. It was sugary sweet, full of delicious calories.

"Last June." He nodded. "My wife died six months ago. Cancer. It's been a helluva year."

"I'm so sorry." Ginny licked cherry filling off her fingers. The tart was still warm from the oven, much better than any McDonald's apple pie would have been. Not that she was picky these days. "I lost my mom to cancer."

"Fuck cancer." He narrowed his rheumy eyes and shook his head.

Ginny blinked at him in surprise. She'd never heard a teacher swear before, but then again, they weren't in school.

"Yeah." She swallowed, smiling grimly, thinking of her mom. "Fuck cancer."

"Are you anorexic, Virginia?"

"Are you kidding me?" She gaped at him, nearly choking on the last of her cherry pie. "Haven't you been watching me eat?"

"Girls these days, I hear they do that." He shrugged. "Starve themselves. It's a strange malady, given the excesses of our culture."

"No, Mr. Spencer. I'm not anorexic." She licked her cherry-stained lips and gulped her cherry Coke.

"You're very thin, Virginia."

She didn't have an answer to that. She knew she was thin. Even before she ran away, there'd only been food at the house sporadically. When Brody felt like leaving grocery money, she went shopping. She ate a lot of boxed mac and cheese and ramen because it was cheap and she could hide it in her room. On the few occasions she tried to get a job, Brody had quashed that, one way or another.

"So are you, Mr. Spencer," she pointed out.

"True." He chuckled, looking down at his thin frame. He wasn't eighty, not really—but his hair was white, the lines in his face deep. "Losing your spouse is an effective diet plan, but I don't recommend it."

"Mr. Spencer, do you have a car?"

"Yes, young lady, I do." He nodded toward the bank. "Left it over there in the parking lot. Why do you ask?"

"I kind of need a ride."

It was too much, she knew. Too risky. What if he told someone—someone who knew Brody? But now that she was full, and warm, that little bit of comfort made her dread trying to find a ride back to Lewisonville. Besides, it was a long shot.

"Sure," Mr. Spencer agreed amiably enough. "You live over on Maple, don't you?"

Crap. How did he remember that?

"Actually... I need a ride to Lewisonville"

"What are you doing in Lewisonville?"

"My sister lives there." That wasn't a lie, not exactly.

"Ah, I remember Maggie." He gave her a knowing nod. "Terrible at algebra."

"She's married. Has two little boys now," Ginny replied. "Doesn't need algebra anymore."

"You always need algebra."

"It's okay. I can take the bus." She couldn't. She didn't have the money. But he didn't need to know that. "I just... don't have a ticket yet..."

"Ah, what the hell. I'm not doing anything for the rest of my life. Let's take a road trip, Virginia."

"Really?" She brightened. "That would be great. Really great!"

"So you said. I have to use the facilities." Mr. Spencer got up slowly. "Be grateful you'll never have a prostate problem, Virginia."

"Okay." She tried to suppress a smile and couldn't. "Actually, I should try to go, too."

She had just started to slide out of the booth when she felt something prickle at the back of her neck. A warning. But what? Mr. Spencer was harmless—she was sure of that.

"Want to meet me at my car?" The old man stood, nodding across the street. It was after five now and the bank lot was empty. They'd all gone home for the day. "It's the white Sable."

"Sure," she agreed, her voice sounding faint, even to her own ears.

She couldn't shake that feeling as she stood and glanced around the coffee shop. She didn't recognize anyone, although most of the tables and booths were filled. Mr. Spencer had already disappeared into the men's room.

That's when she felt him watching her. It wasn't so much seeing him as just knowing, a kind of extrasensory jolt. Her gaze lifted to see Brody staring at her through the frosted glass window. She bolted from the booth and straight-armed the door, heading in the opposite direction from Brody, trying not to run and attract attention to her flight. When she glanced behind her, she saw his wiry frame threading through the crowd of Christmas shoppers, his uniform parting the tide.

He caught her in the alleyway and she realized her mistake the moment his hand found her neck and pressed her, face first, hard against the brick. There was no one back here, no bright lights, no warm bodies—no watching eyes. It was cold, dark, and they were completely alone.

"Did you think you could run from me?" Brody's breath reeked of alcohol, even though he was wearing his uniform, and Ginny turned her head, struggling. "Did you really think you could hide?"

She couldn't answer. His hand at her throat made it impossible. He wasn't a big man, but he was tall and sinewy, and surprisingly strong. His voice turned smooth as he took his hand from her throat, twisting her arm up behind her, his weight pressing her into the wall.

"I told you, girl." His voice was like slick oil against her ear. "You can't ever hide from me. I own the system. Don't forget it. You're a number that shows up wherever you go. I've got eyes everywhere. You rent a motel room, you're mine. You use a credit card, you're mine. Put your name on a lease, you're mine. You get a paycheck, you're mine. Do you understand me? *You. Are. Mine.*"

Ginny gave in to her fear—no matter what she did, no matter where she ran, he would track her down. She nearly gasped out loud at her own realization. Hot tears stung her eyes and she looked away, down the alley, hoping to see someone, anyone. There was nothing but darkness. She cursed her hunger, the driving need that had allowed her to accept Mr. Spencer's invitation to the little café when Brody just happened to be passing by.

He felt her relenting and let up a little, taking the opportunity to ask conversationally, "So where is it, Gin? Just give it to me and we'll be done. I promise you."

"Why didn't you find me weeks ago?" she taunted. She felt him startle, could almost hear the frown when he grunted and tightened his grip. "If you're so smart, so *connected*..."

"Shut up!" he growled, making her wince when he shoved his knee between hers, pressing her belly into the wall.

"I don't have it with me," she lied flatly, aching to hide or ditch her bag somewhere, using all of her force of will to keep still and let its weight dangle from her forearm, as if she couldn't care less. "But if you touch me... if you touch anyone I care about... your face will be all over the news, and this time it won't be because the mayor is pinning a ribbon to your chest."

"Bullshit!" He didn't sound convinced. She felt him hesitating, his breath short and struggling in her ear.

"No," Ginny said, surprising herself with the steel edge in her voice. "You're the bullshit artist, Brody. Me, I tell the truth, and I'm telling you the truth right now. Believe it."

The back door swung open and Ginny recognized one of the café workers as he brought out a bag of trash. His eyes widened in surprise and he looked concerned—before he saw Brody's uniform, anyway. Ginny knew how much power that uniform had, how it could immediately anesthetize.

"Thank you, Officer," Ginny gasped, using the moment of surprise to twist out of Brody's grip and head toward the young man still standing agape in the doorway. "You saved my life."

"Hey!" Brody called, but he was too late. She was already disappearing through the busy coffee house and out the front door onto the street.

She hid, cowering behind the McDonalds dumpster, for a good five minutes. Maybe ten. She was too afraid to even move, sure Brody would come around the corner and find her any moment. Then she remembered Mr. Spencer and her promise to meet him at his car. Had he already driven away?

Ginny dared to peek out from behind the dumpster and saw his white car in the lot. There was exhaust coming from the back end, so he was in it. Did she dare? It was only the thought that Brody would be looking for her, that he wouldn't give up now that he'd sighted her, that finally got her moving. The faster she got away from this town, the better, and Mr. Spencer was her fastest way out at the moment.

"And I thought I took a long time in the bathroom," Mr. Spencer said when Ginny pulled the car door open and threw herself into the car. "You don't have prostate problems, do you?"

"No," she panted. "I've got ninety-nine other problems, but that's not one. Step on it, Mr. Spencer."

"Why, are the cops after you?"

"No." That wasn't a complete lie. There was just one cop after her.

Ginny sank low in the passenger seat as Mr. Spencer pulled slowly out onto the street, like any senior citizen driver would. It was far less *Fast and Furious* than she wanted it to be, but she didn't see any sign of Brody. Still, she didn't fully relax until they got out of town and onto the highway. Mr. Spencer was doing a measly fifty-five—and at that rate, it would be three hours before they got into Lewisonville—but the heater was on and, with every mile, she got further and further way from Brody.

That was a blessed relief.

"What do you think, Virginia?" Mr. Spencer asked, pulling a CD out of a sleeve on his visor. "Creedence or Bruce Springsteen?"

She wasn't about to ask him if he had anything more current or, perhaps, an iPod.

"Creedence," she decided, taking the CD from him and sliding it into the player. It was full dark already and there was a moon rising. She just hoped it wasn't a bad one, like the song said.

"Mr. Spencer, do you mind if I take a nap?" she murmured, but her eyes were already closing as she leaned her head against the window.

"Not at all, Virginia," he said, but his voice already sounded far away. "Not at all."

Maggie and the boys were already outside when she showed up at the shelter but the boys weren't on the swings. It had snowed overnight, and they were running and playing in the white stuff, throwing snowballs, making snow angels and sliding on the ice. There was a big hill out back that crested into a golf course on the other side—there was a big fence at the top—and Ginny found herself wishing they had a sled.

"You look tired." Maggie, always the little mother hen, touched Ginny's cheek, her hand moving to her forehead, as if she was checking for a fever. "Are you okay?"

"I'm fine, Mags." Ginny unslung her backpack and dropped it onto an ice patch. Her shoulders ached from carrying it everywhere, although she was finally starting to get used to it.

"Did you get a chance to go to the bank?" Maggie asked, shading her eyes against the sun—it was bright, but the day was too cold to allow for much melt—to see what the boys were up to, when Michael let out a war whoop and took off after his brother.

"I..." Ginny swallowed, the memory of the bank visit and her near-miss with Brody still fresh in her mind. Thank God for Mr. Spencer and his lonely longing for someone to talk to for a while, or she would likely be in Brody's dangerous and unpredictable company as they spoke.

"Damnit, Ginny!" Maggie sighed and shook her head. "I need that money! I've got to get a place for the boys before Christmas. Will you please try to be a grown-up for five minutes and take some responsibility for once? You're not always going to be able to draw pretty rainbow ponies and pretend the real world doesn't exist!"

Ginny didn't say anything as she watched the boys tumble into a snowbank, laughing and tussling, shrieking in that high-pitched tone only kids seemed to be able to hit when they were young. She remembered doing that with Maggie, when they were little kids. Her older sister liked to grab the back of Ginny's head and rub her face in it. They called it a "face-wash." They weren't mean to each other, but they were siblings, after all.

Once Brody came along, though, they found themselves banding together in ways they never had before. And after their mom was gone, Maggie became the little mother out of necessity. She was always telling Ginny to grow up, be responsible, practical. Art school wasn't practical, of course. Art school was a pipe dream that was never going to get her out from under Brody's thumb.

"I'm sorry, Mags." Ginny swallowed again, the words coming out slowly. She didn't want to have to tell her sister that her addict husband had emptied not only their bank account, but their safe deposit box too. She didn't want to tell her a lot of things. It was better that Maggie kept thinking she was living at home, untouched by Brody, untouched by the rest of the world and its very cold shoulder.

"You always say you're sorry." Maggie scowled, crossing her arms over her chest. It reminded Ginny of the lectures she used to get in high school for her grades. Brody didn't seem to care about school, as long as they weren't truant or in trouble. C's were fine for Brody. But not for Maggie. She constantly pushed Ginny to get A's. Even a B+ was cause for alarm.

Of course, Ginny was glad now. She'd made it through high school with a 3.8 GPA average. Geometry had been her nemesis. Algebra she understood. Trig was easy. But geometry? Nope. The good news was that her transcripts were amazing. She could apply at any college in the country and have a good shot at getting in. That just created another point of contention between the sisters—Maggie wanted Ginny to go to a good school and choose a smart, profitable profession.

You could be a lawyer, a doctor, anything, Ginny! Just don't be a goddamned artist.

But Ginny knew her sister was speaking from the land of lost opportunities. Maggie was looking back at her own high school career of skipping classes and going out with boys and generally goofing off until she found herself just a little bit pregnant. Not that Ginny could blame her. Maggie had kept her secret from her younger sister as long as she could. She probably never would have confessed it, if Ginny hadn't actually seen it for herself one afternoon when she'd come home from school sick with the flu and found her sister bent over the kitchen table, Brody rutting behind her like an animal.

"Boys!" Maggie called, giving that helpless cross-armed wave Ginny always associated with people trying to flag down planes from deserted islands. "Come on in now!"

"I thought I'd go out back and see if I could find a box for them to make into a sled," Ginny said with a frown as the boys looked back at their mother, both wearing identical frowns.

"Don't come back until you've gone to the bank, Ginny." Maggie took a little hand in each of hers as the boys trudged back and stopped beside her. "I'll see you later."

Ginny watched her sister and her nephews head back into the shelter, feeling the weight of her own secrets weighing heavily on her chest. It constricted her throat, making it impossible to speak, to call after them. She couldn't tell her, didn't want to see the look of disappointment on Maggie's face. It was better Maggie thought she was just an irresponsible kid.

Yes, she would tell her—she would have to. Eventually. But for now, she let her sister and the boys go into the shelter, swallowing her own disappointment and sorrow before turning and walking away, her tears making her cheeks sting, another sharp punishment in the bitter cold she was willing to bear to keep her sister blissfully ignorant just a little bit longer.

Chapter Four

She practically lived at the library. They had a "reading loft" for the kids. Some woodworking parent had built it with raised platforms covered with different colored remnants of carpet so the kids could get up there and read to their heart's content. She could easily still pass for fourteen or fifteen, so they didn't mind her in the kids' section. She'd fallen asleep at the top of the reading loft quite a few times, although she was usually drawing instead of reading. The librarian was a nice old guy—not as old as Mr. Spencer, but everyone over forty seemed "old" to her—who didn't seem to care if she came in every day. She wished she could sleep all night in the loft, but the one time she'd tried, the librarian—his name tag said, *"Ask Me For Help - Dale Knoffler"*—had woken her up and told her she had to go home.

But she couldn't go home. Which meant, she didn't have anywhere else to go. At least, not until after Christmas. The "underground railroad" network she'd found kind of shut down over the holidays, because so many people were busy and they were already stuffed to the gills with visiting family members. And, according to the woman she'd talked to via web chat on the library's computer, they needed time to process her and find families to take her in. She was in the process of "being processed" and the woman—her web name was KitKat247, but Ginny just thought of her as "Kit"—checked in with her via Gmail.

She was thrilled to discover another email from Kit that evening. The library was open until ten—that's what she said when a doubtful Mr. Spencer dropped her off there the other day, telling him she was meeting a friend—which made it a great place to spend a lot of time. And people didn't care, as long as you were quiet.

Dale wasn't working—there was a different librarian at night, a younger woman with short, dark hair who dressed in cardigans and skirts—so Ginny went straight for the computers and avoided the front desk. She checked her email and discovered the letter from KitKat247, affirming that there was a family in Ohio who could take her in between Christmas and New Year's.

After that, her spirits lifted. The trip back to her home town had really shaken her. If Mr. Spencer hadn't been there to offer her a ride home, Brody probably would have found her. That thought made her sick to her stomach. She didn't like to imagine what would happen if Brody caught her. He wouldn't just be content taking the SD memory card from her. He'd want to take far, far more than that, as punishment.

Ginny went into the children's section of the library and climbed up into the loft. There was one kid there, a girl about ten or twelve, reading a manga book. They glanced at each other and smiled in acknowledgement as Ginny passed her, climbing higher into the loft, to the very top. It was warm up there—there was a vent right above her head—and she wished she could stock up on warm air the way she had stocked up on food in her belly at the coffee shop with Mr. Spencer.

The poor old guy was so lonely, he'd agreed to take a four-hour round-trip just to have someone to talk to for a few hours. Ginny had apologized for not having enough money to pay him, even for gas, but he just shook his head, pulling a money clip out of his pocket. She'd watched, feeling humiliated and awful, as he unclipped it and peeled off a ten-dollar-bill.

"Mr. Spencer, I can't..." she protested. But she'd taken his money, realizing she could eat on that for a few days, if she was careful. That, and the peanut butter in her pocket, was the highlight of the day.

Well, and Mr. Spencer's last words to her before he pulled away.

"Take care of yourself, Virginia," he had called, rolling down the passenger window so she could hear him as she headed toward the library. "You're a smart girl. You have a bright future ahead of you. That's a light at the end of the tunnel, not a train. I promise."

She certainly hoped so.

Ginny took out her sketch pad and half-heartedly worked on her Wolverine drawing, but she couldn't concentrate. Brody was on her mind. He was always working in the back of her mind, and fear kept her motivated—the memory of his hand at her throat, the snarl of his words in her ear.

I'm everywhere.

He was right, of course. She was terrified he was going to find her. She was even more terrified he was going to find Maggie and the boys. She knew her being anywhere near them put them all in jeopardy, but she didn't know where else to go. *At least he thinks I'm still in town*, she realized, remembering the surprised look in his eyes when he'd seen her sitting in the coffee shop. Now he'd be looking around town still, at least, instead of casting his net wider. That made her feel a little safer.

And she'd survived. She'd faced him down, and she'd survived. She'd even gotten away!

Ginny's belly was overly full, the loft was blessedly warm, and her eyes were too heavy to keep open. She closed them in relief, sure she'd dream about the constant threat of Brody, but it wasn't him she was thinking about as she drifted off. It was the stranger, the one she kept seeing around town, the one she didn't know but who looked oddly familiar. Was he really a private detective? Was he reporting to Brody?

He'd talked to her today for the first time. She remembered that encounter, squirming at the memory of her own awkwardness. She couldn't trust him, that much she knew. She didn't dare let herself trust anyone.

It wasn't the librarian who woke her—it was the little girl. She stuck her head up like a gopher and said, "Hey, the library's closing." Ginny sighed, packing her sketch book back into her bag and slowly climbing down from the warm, comfortable loft. It would be a cold, fifteen-minute trek back to the strip mall. She couldn't go into the video store vestibule until after midnight, so she still had two hours to kill. Usually, she sat behind the store, drawing in the light of the street lamp.

At least Maggie and the boys are safe and warm, Ginny thought as she used the library's bathroom—it would be her last opportunity before morning. She re-tied her hair with the Scrunchie, glad to have it. It would make walking in the cold so much better. And she had ten dollars in her pocket. That thought made her feel a little warmer as she put her backpack on and headed out.

"Goodnight!"

Ginny turned to see the little girl leaving and waved at her. The girl's mother was leading the way to their car—the only one left in the lot, besides what Ginny assumed was the librarian's. They were going home, of course, and some part of her wished she was, too. Maybe not home to Brody—that had never felt like home, at least, not after Maggie left—but some home, somewhere.

What would it be like to have a real home?

It was silly, but she'd fantasized on the drive back into town about telling Mr. Spencer her plight, asking him to take her in. But she was too old to be adopted, too old to be looking for a mother, a father, a home. She was going to have to make those things for herself, some day. And she was working on it, as hard as she could.

At least, she thought, turning her back to the mother and daughter pair, *I'm not living with Brody anymore.*

Ginny consoled herself with that thought and started her walk toward the only home she had—a six-by-six square that was actually less of a cage than anything she'd ever lived in before.

"Where did all these people come from?" Ginny asked Robbie as she put her backpack down on the only empty café table she could find.

"Book signing!" was all he said as he practically ran by, heading for the food counter. They had two other people working there and the line was still all the way to the door.

She took a seat, realizing she wasn't likely to get any food from Robbie—he was too busy, and there were far too many people. Her ten dollars was burning a hole in her pocket, and her stomach growled. It amazed her how quickly the human body decided it needed fuel again. *Maybe someone will leave something*, she thought, glancing around at the tables filled with packages and plates. There wasn't an empty chair in the place, except for the one across from her.

"Do you mind?" The voice startled her, and Ginny looked up to meet those smiling brown eyes, the same ones she'd met yesterday coming out of the Barnes & Noble bathroom. "This place is packed and I'm pretty sure this is the only empty seat."

"Um..." Ginny stumbled over her words, trying to find some. Instead, she just shook her head, but when the man took a seat, she realized he'd interpreted the shake of her head to mean that she didn't mind if he sat. Because he did sit, turning the chair backwards and straddling it. He was wearing khakis and a navy-blue jacket His eyes were bright as he looked at her over the surface of the table. Ginny hugged her backpack to her, glancing toward the counter, where Robbie was taking someone's order.

"Hungry?" The man pulled a banana and two chocolate chip cookies wrapped in plastic out of one pocket, and a Diet Coke out of the other. "I'll share."

"Um..." She swallowed, feeling her heart racing. Was he playing with her? Toying, like a cat with a mouse? The more she looked at him, the more she was sure he was some kind of cop. "I don't..."

"Cookie or banana?"

She couldn't remember the last time she had fresh fruit. But she couldn't take anything from him. She definitely couldn't talk to him. Anything she said could and would be used against her—she was sure of it.

He put the cookie and the banana on the table, closer to her than to him. Then he opened the tab on the can of soda and gulped some down. But his gaze never left her. She watched him unwrap the other chocolate chip cookie and break off a piece. He chewed it, looking thoughtfully at her, and she wondered what he was thinking.

"Are you here for the book signing?"

Ginny shook her head. The less she talked to him the better, as far as she was concerned. She was going to have to abandon the idea of spending the afternoon in Barnes & Noble for the day and head over to the library.

"They hired me to do security." He was making small talk. And it was just a distraction, she realized. He looked at her like he was sizing her up. Trying to make sense of her.

"Shouldn't you be working?" Maybe reminding him would give her the opportunity to slip out. The fact that he was working security detail just served to prove her right. She just knew he was some kind of P.I. She wouldn't be surprised if he'd been hired by Brody to gather intel on her.

"Lunch break." He leaned over his chair, looking at her. He reminded her of someone, but she couldn't quite identify who. His sandy brown hair and dark, brown eyes were nondescript, but he was a good-looking guy. He had that going for him. And the biceps showing under his tight-fitting black t-shirt told her he worked out. A lot. Which would jive with her feeling that he was a cop. "Not your usual quiet day at the book store, huh?"

She startled at his words. My God, he'd practically just admitted he was following and watching her!

"I have to go," she murmured, shouldering her backpack. Just being in his presence threw everything off. She didn't know why—maybe just her suspicions—but he made her feel hot and cold at the same time.

"Do you want to meet the author?" He raised his eyebrows at her in question as she stood. It was a nice offer, maybe even a real one, but she wanted to get as far away from this place as fast as she possibly good.

"No." She gave him a wan smile. "I... I have to go."

"Not a Chloe Clay fan?"

She was already starting to walk away when his words stopped her.

"Who?" she breathed, not quite believing her own ears, glancing over her shoulder at him. "*Who* did you say?"

"I would have thought, the way you draw..." He nodded toward her backpack where her sketch books were tucked away. She didn't like the way he knew things about her.

"Chloe Clay is... here?" Ginny blinked at him in disbelief. It couldn't be. Could it?

He nodded. "The book signing. Want to meet her?"

What could she say to that? It was a once in a lifetime opportunity. She felt like someone had just stepped up and offered her a million dollars. She looked around like Ed McMahon had just knocked on her door with a giant check.

"I... yes." She couldn't say no. Even if this guy was someone Brody had hired, she couldn't say no. She knew she'd been distracted, but how had she missed that Chloe Clay was coming to Barnes and Noble? She was here practically every day! Why hadn't Robbie mentioned it?

"So, you *are* a fan?"

"I... yes." She slanted her eyes at the brown-haired stranger, reaching down to put the banana and cookie into her coat pocket. Was he putting her on? "Is Chloe Clay really here?"

"Where have you been?" He laughed, pulling something out of his pocket and putting it on the table. Ginny glanced at the flyer, seeing her favorite author and artist's smiling photo. "Come on, I'll sneak you in."

Well, he was telling the truth about the book signing, anyway. Ginny followed him toward the back of the store. They had to weave their way through a crowd of people. When she looked up, she noticed it— a banner with Chloe Clay's face on it with that day's date. She had seen the banner before, but hadn't really paid attention to the date, or that it advertised a book signing. She knew Chloe's new graphic novel was out this month, and maybe subconsciously she'd been ignoring it, because she knew she couldn't afford the damned thing, and it would be six months before she could check it out of the library, even though she'd put her name on the waiting list two months ago.

"Are you sure we should be...?" she whispered, tugging on his sleeve as he opened a door marked *Employees Only*. The man's bicep was like rock.

"It's fine." He winked down at her as they slipped through the door. "She already signed a book for me. I'm sure she's bored back here..."

"You got that right." Chloe Clay looked up from her Kindle, taking off the turquoise pair of reading glasses perched on her nose. She was a chubby woman, compact, wearing a rather unflattering navy pant suit, her dark hair pulled up into a messy bun—but she was the most beautiful sight Ginny had ever seen. "Have you ended lunch early to come keep me company, Nick?"

"No, ma'am..." Nick flushed at the way the author looked at him. Not that Ginny blamed her, in a way. The man was easy on the eyes. "I mean, I just wanted to introduce you to..."

"Ma'am?" Chloe scoffed, closing her Kindle case with a snap. "I'm sorry, ma'am is my mother. Or my grandmother. Who's this little waif?"

"This is..."

"Ginny." She said her real name without even thinking about it until it was too late. "Virginia."

"Hello, Virginia." Chloe Clay stood and held out her hand, and Ginny took it. She couldn't believe she was shaking the woman's hand! "Any friend of Nick's here is a friend of mine."

She realized, too late, that she'd just given Nick her name. Nothing like doing the man's job for him! She could have kicked herself. What was she thinking? She'd been so damned careful so far! Now, faced with her favorite author, she went all star-struck and stupid.

"I'm a huge fan of your work," Ginny told the woman. That was the understatement of the year, to say the least. "I've read everything. Just everything. Even the Starcrossed Trilogy."

"Even that old thing? You must be a big fan." Chloe laughed, taking her seat again, crossing her legs. "Do you have something you'd like me to sign?"

Ginny's face fell. All her books were at home. She'd had to leave anything she couldn't carry, and books were heavy. Especially graphic novels, thick with illustrations, like Chloe wrote. She'd read them all to death, anyway.

"Ummm..." Ginny blinked at the woman, feeling stupid. There was a stack of books on the table beside her, and she realized it was Chloe's latest. It had just released that day.

"It's okay. I can just sign one of these." Chloe reached for one of the books from the stack, opening the front page. "To Ginny?"

"Oh, no... I don't... I mean... I can't..." She thought of the ten dollars in her pocket, but that wouldn't even cover it. One of those graphic novels was at least twenty bucks. Usually more.

"It's okay," Nick said softly at her elbow. "I'm buying."

"No, really, I can't..." She glanced up at him, into those kind, brown eyes, frowning. She didn't like him being so nice to her.

"A little advice." Chloe was already writing her name in the book. "When a young man as handsome as this one offers to buy... you don't say no."

"Thank you," Ginny managed, taking the book from her. Not only did she have a copy of Chloe Clay's new book in her hand, it was now autographed. She couldn't quite believe it.

"Ginny's an artist, you know," Nick said, making Ginny feel like she wanted the floor to open and swallow her whole. "She's really good. Show her."

"Oh... no..." Ginny felt the heat filling her face and hoped it wasn't as obvious as it felt. "I'm sure she doesn't want to look at some amateur's drawings."

"Let me see." Chloe's smile was perfunctory as she held out her hand.

Ginny knew the woman was doing it because she thought Nick was a hottie. She wasn't really interested in Ginny or her drawings. Ginny couldn't figure out why that bothered her so much—she didn't expect Chloe Clay to consider her at all—but it did.

"A little advice—when a famous artist asks to see your drawings, you don't say no." Nick nudged her, and Ginny glanced up at him, frowning. "Show her the Wolverine you did. It's amazing."

Nick was looking at her and Chloe was holding out her hand, and Ginny couldn't do anything but unsling her backpack and slide out one of her sketch books.

"These are just..." Ginny handed it over, reluctant. "I'm doing these as coloring books. For my nephews. For Christmas."

"Nice detail." Chloe flipped through it but didn't seem that interested, Ginny could tell by the way her eyes passed over the drawings. "Do you have anything else? Anything original?"

"Well..." Many of her paintings had been far too big to carry with her and she'd left them back at Brody's. But she did have one thing. "These are mine."

She took out another sketch book from her backpack. The coiled end caught on a pair of her panties and they went flying, hitting Nick square in the chest. Ginny had never been so mortified in her life. They fell to the floor at his feet and he bent to retrieve them. Thankfully, Chloe hadn't seemed to notice. She was already flipping through the sketch book Ginny handed to her.

Nick didn't say anything—he just handed Ginny's panties back. She shoved them down deep into her bag, trying to ignore the heat in her cheeks as she stood, watching Chloe peruse drawings Ginny had never shown anyone—not even her art teacher in high school. Chloe didn't say anything as she slowly flipped the pages. She lingered on some, flipped past others. Ginny couldn't tell what she was thinking.

Interested, Nick peered over the woman's shoulder, watching her turn the pages. Ginny still couldn't get over the fact that the man had been holding a pair of her panties just moments before. She also couldn't quite grasp that she was not only standing before Chloe Clay, but the woman had given her not only her autograph, and was now looking through her own personal version of a graphic novel. She'd been working on it for a few years, so the earlier drawings were more rudimentary. Ginny noticed Chloe slowing down as she turned the pages.

"Hey, I didn't finish," Nick protested when the author closed the book halfway through.

"That's the sign of talent, girl." Chloe winked as she handed Ginny back her pad. "He wants to keep reading."

"Thank you." Ginny shoved it into her backpack, not quite sure how to take the compliment.

"How old are you?" Chloe asked, eyes narrowing at her, speculative.

"Almost nineteen."

"Going to school?"

"I want to go to art school."

"Well, let me know if you want to skip the debt." Chloe rolled her eyes, reaching into a bag beside her and pulling out a card. "Seriously. If you're ever in New York, look me up. I'll introduce you to some people. Bring that with you."

"I... okay." Ginny wasn't quite sure what to say. The truth was, she was going in the opposite direction. California was as far from New York as she could get—in this country, anyway.

"Can I have a word, Ms. Clay?" The *Employees Only* door swung open and Ginny recognized the manager of the store. She tried to avoid him as much as possible, worried he would think she was always loitering. He didn't even notice her, although she did her best to hide her presence behind Nick's solid bulk.

"Sure." Chloe stood up, brushing off her pant suit. "Nice to meet you, Virginia."

"You too," Ginny replied. She had to say it. "Thank you so much."

Chloe and the manager were already talking, and Ginny followed Nick out into the store.

Chapter Five

"Thank you," Ginny said as they weaved their way toward the front of the store. "For introducing me. For the book."

"Want to get some lunch? I mean, some real lunch—not the cookie and banana in your pocket." He dropped her a wink as they reached the café up front.

"Oh, you can have them back..." She flushed, reaching into her pocket.

"Keep them, Ginny." He laughed. "Do you want a sandwich to go with them?"

Of course, she did—but she wasn't sure spending more time with him was such a good idea. She still wasn't quite sure of the man's motives, even if she was starting to doubt her original theory.

"I am a little hungry," she confessed.

"All right, now we're talking." A family was getting up from one of the tables and Nick grabbed it, nodding at the opposite chair. "You stay here. What do you want? Tuna? Chicken salad?"

"Ham and cheese," she replied, remembering yesterday's coffee shop sandwich. Two sandwiches in as many days! It was like a Christmas miracle. "And a chocolate milk?"

"You got it." He dropped her a rather sexy wink and she felt that hot and cold feeling again. Maybe she'd been wrong to distrust him after all? "You're going to be here when I get back, right? You're not going to disappear?"

"Not if you're coming back with sandwiches." She grinned. She couldn't help it.

She watched Nick standing in line, thinking about her original private detective theory. Maybe he wasn't what he seemed? She had that cop-vibe from him—she could smell it a mile away—but perhaps that was just because he worked in security? And, even if Lewisonville wasn't as small as Millsberg, it was still a pretty small town. So, she'd seen him around—was that really that strange? She was more than a little paranoid, she knew, given her circumstances.

Maybe the handsome stranger was just that—a handsome stranger. Maybe he looked at her because—well, she wasn't going to entertain that thought. She couldn't afford to be thinking about things like cute guys at a time like this. If she wanted to think about cute guys, she would have taken Robbie up on his offer of TV dinners the other night. Robbie was cute enough, if kind of nerdy. She just couldn't let any guy out of the friend-zone right now.

But this guy, this Nick—even Chloe Clay, twice their age, had caught scent of the man's excess testosterone. She guessed he was probably a little older than she was, but not much. Still, he seemed older. He acted older. Maybe that was what Chloe Clay was picking up on. Or maybe it was the biceps, the cleft in his chin, the dazzling smile and the bright brown eyes? And Ginny didn't even want to know if the woman had noticed the way the man's jeans fit him like a second skin.

It wasn't easy to resist a guy like that, especially when he winked at you. And glanced over to make sure you were still sitting at the table where he left you. And bought you ham and cheese sandwiches and chocolate milk. Chloe Clay had made it pretty clear—even in front of Ginny—that Nick could butter her muffin if he wanted to, but here he was, buying Ginny lunch. She couldn't help feeling a little smug about that.

Ginny saw Robbie frowning at her across the counter as Nick paid for their food. She knew he was concerned, and she was still concerned, too, a little. But the more she considered Nick and his actions, the more she thought her own paranoia had gotten the better of her. She didn't know who he was, but maybe she could finally find out, once and for all.

Nick came back and put their sandwiches on the table, along with a small bag of kettle chips, another Diet Coke, and her bottle of chocolate milk.

"Thank you," she said through a mouth full of ham and cheese, already digging in. He watched her, looking amused. "I keep seeing you around..."

It was the best she could do, without coming out directly and asking him.

"Same here." He gave her a rueful smile. "Small town."

Ginny chewed her sandwich thoughtfully. It wasn't as good as the coffee house sandwich had been—or maybe, after having a ham and cheese sandwich two whole days in a row, she was already becoming jaded—but her stomach was grateful, nonetheless.

"How old are you?" she wondered aloud.

"Twenty-two." He took a swig of his Diet Coke, confirming her suspicions. Not much older than her. "You're eighteen?"

"Almost nineteen." She opened her chocolate milk, drinking out of the carton.

"When's your birthday?" he asked.

"...June." She took another swig of milk, flushing.

"Almost." He grinned, making air quotes with his fingers.

"Close enough." She stuck her tongue out at him and he laughed.

"You're really very talented," he said, making her flush even more. "It's not fair to all the other girls, you know."

"Being talented?" She rolled her eyes.

"Being that talented *and* so beautiful."

Now she was really blushing for real. Guys flirting with her was nothing new—but this guy was different. She knew he was flirting, but he was serious, too. There was something in his eyes, an honesty, that was surprising.

"Do all the girls fall for that line?" she scoffed, licking mustard off her fingers.

"Every single one so far." He grinned.

"They didn't tell you? I'm the exception to the rule." She rolled her eyes again, wiping her mouth with a napkin from one of the dispensers on the table.

"They broke the mold, did they?"

"Yep," she agreed. "And a bunch of other clichés."

"Are you playing hard to get?" He took another swig of Diet Coke.

"No," she replied honestly. "I am hard to get. Just ask Robbie over there."

"I don't think Robbie ever had a shot." Nick glanced over his shoulder at Robbie, who was still watching them with a dark look on his face. "He couldn't handle a girl like you."

"Don't tell him that." Ginny laughed. "Hey, what does that mean?"

"You're a handful." Nick looked at her like he knew. How could he know?

"How would you know?"

"I'm afraid my break's up." He shrugged, but he was smiling as he glanced at his watch. "Do you want my sandwich? I don't have time."

He slid it across the table toward her.

"You can leave it," she replied, trying to sound casual.

The man had been a fountain of wealth for her that afternoon, between the cookie, the banana, lunch, and now his own sandwich—not to mention the autographed book and the opportunity to meet her favorite author!

"Nice seeing you again, Ginny."

"You too." She watched him walk away, frowning. She still had far too many questions about him than answers, and she didn't like it.

She hadn't hung around Barnes and Noble after that. She didn't think being around Nick was a good idea—and from the way Robbie glowered at her, she knew she was likely in for a talking-to. Instead, she'd spent the afternoon at the library in the loft, going through her sketches and thinking about what Chloe Clay had said. Had she really meant it? Or was that a line she gave all the budding artists she met?

The card Chloe had given her wasn't a personal one—it was to the Morrow Agency. Presumably Chloe's agent? But maybe she could be contacted through them. She imagined calling and asking for Chloe Clay, imagined the laughter on the other end of the phone. Yeah, it was just a line, she decided, probably inspired by the older woman's raging hormones and desire to get into Nick-the-hot-security-guard's pants.

When the library closed, she walked back to the video store, noticing that Dunkin' Donuts was still open. They had extended hours during the holidays, probably hoping shoppers would stop in to warm up with coffee and donuts. She could use a little of her ten dollars to buy a small drink and stay there for an hour, until eleven, and then wait in the cold until after midnight before creeping into the video store vestibule to try to get some sleep. Thankfully, she'd caught up a little on her sleep deficit in the library loft that afternoon.

Ginny had just slid into a booth when the door opened, the bell over it dinging. She glanced up, seeing the flash of a blue uniform and a badge, her heart jumping in her chest. Every time she saw a uniform, that happened. She was always afraid it was going to be Brody—or one of Brody's many cop friends.

This time, though, it was just Nick.

She'd been right after all. Nick was a cop.

He hadn't seen her yet, and she thought about side-stepping into the bathroom, but knew it would just draw more attention to herself. Maybe he would just go out without...

"Ginny?" He gave her a bemused smile, coming over to her booth.

"Are you following me again?" she asked, trying to sound annoyed as she sipped her milk. It was white milk this time, but full-fat. It helped make her feel full.

"Um..." He pointed at his badge and then up at the sign—*Dunkin' Donuts*—grinning.

"Are you telling me that stereotype is true?" She smirked.

"They have to come from somewhere."

"You're really getting donuts?"

"Actually, I'm getting coffee." He laughed. "Want something?"

"Umm..." She looked at her milk, then at him. It was hard to turn down free food, but she knew accepting would just encourage him, and she wasn't so sure she wanted to do that.

"I think they sell ham and cheese sandwiches," he said, tempting her.

"No." She shook her head, waving him away. "Thanks, anyway."

"You sure?" He glanced back at her over his shoulder as he neared the counter again. The girl working had full sleeve tattoos, a nose stud, and wore her black hair, with lightning streaks of blue, pulled back into a ponytail.

"Can I help you?" she asked, looking Nick up and down in his uniform. Not that he didn't look good in it—he did, Ginny had to admit.

"I'll take a hot chocolate," Ginny called out toward the counter. "And a bear claw… and maybe an éclair?"

"Anything else?" Nick grinned over his shoulder at her.

"No, that's it." Ginny's cheeks grew pink when the goth girl gave her a knowing look.

"Cream or custard?" Nick asked when he gave the girl Ginny's order.

"Custard," Ginny piped up.

"Good choice." Nick pulled out his wallet, turning back to the tattooed girl. "I'll also take a large coffee, black. Oh, and a raspberry jelly filled."

She rang it all up and put it in a tray that Nick carried over to Ginny's booth.

"Aren't you on duty?" she asked as he slid in across from her, already biting into her éclair.

"Small town, remember?" He opened the steam vent on the top of his coffee and patted his belt. "Anyway, I've got my radio."

"I knew you were a cop." She looked at him speculatively, licking custard off her fingers.

"How did you know?" He raised his eyebrows, looking at her over the rim of his cup.

"You walk like a cop."

"How does a cop walk?" He snorted a laugh.

"Like you own the world." She grabbed a napkin, but it didn't do much for her sticky fingers.

"Cops aren't the bad guys, Ginny," he said softly, frowning. "We're the good guys."

"Uh-huh." She blew on the top of her hot chocolate, cooling it. "So, are you on duty all night?"

The thought of him patrolling the parking lot all night gave her a cold chill. How often had he done that already? She wondered.

"Most of it." He stretched and yawned. He really was a good-looking guy, and she thought he knew it. He saw the way the goth girl looked at him. The way Chloe Clay had practically invited him back to her hotel room. Ginny wasn't about to give him the same satisfaction by fawning all over him. "Good overtime opportunities around the holidays."

"Good for the wallet. Not so great for the family?" she asked, taking a sip of hot chocolate. It was too hot, but delicious. God, she missed chocolate.

"No family."

"No wife?" She looked at him, surprised.

"Nope."

"Girlfriend?" She cocked her head, frowning. She was sure he was married, or at least attached. Most guys would have picked up on the tattooed girl's look. And Chloe Clay's offer had been pretty obvious, even to her.

"Position's open." He smirked.

"I wasn't fishing."

"Sure you were." He laughed. "Maybe not for fish, but you were asking for a reason."

"Cops." Ginny shook her head, rolling her eyes as she drank her hot chocolate.

"What's that mean?"

"You're always interrogating."

"I wasn't the one asking the questions." He grinned. "How about you?"

"Me what?" She glanced over at the goth girl, who was arranging the end-of-the-day donuts on a tray.

"Family?" he inquired, looking more serious. "Husband? Boyfriend?"

"Husband?" Ginny choked on her hot chocolate. "Hardly. No boyfriend either. You're certainly asking questions now!"

"Might as well, since you accused me and all." He had such a great smile. It was hard not to return it. "So, how's Maggie?"

She stopped, staring at him, feeling her whole body go cold.

"Who?" Her mouth felt dry, her eyes hot.

"Your sister—Maggie?" He frowned at the look on her face.

"How do you know...?" She couldn't even finish the sentence. Her hands were shaking and she set her hot chocolate on the table.

"You really don't remember me, do you?" Nick asked, realization dawning in his eyes.

"Should I?" She swallowed, blinking at him.

The radio on his belt went off and Nick frowned down at it.

"Damn, I gotta go." He stood, tipping her a little salute. "I'll see you around, Ginny."

She sat in her chair, dumbfounded, too numb to move. Her limbs refused to respond. What in the hell had just happened? How had he known her sister's name? She knew that, while she had slipped and given him her real name at Barnes and Noble, she'd never told him about her sister.

Had he looked her up? The thought made her want to throw up.

She glanced down at the table and saw that, for the second time in two days, he'd left food for her. His jelly donut was untouched, but he'd taken his coffee with him. Ginny stared after him, watching as he neared his squad car. She'd relaxed a little around him that afternoon, chiding herself that she was being paranoid, but it turned out her instincts had been right on.

He was a cop—and he had pulled her record. Which meant he knew she was a runaway—she had no doubt Brody had reported her as missing, even if she wasn't a minor anymore. Had he called Brody, one cop to another? Was Brody, as she sat there in a Dunkin' Donuts booth, on his way to Lewisonville to collect her right this minute?

Another cop car pulled up beside Nick's and she dropped lower in the booth. She couldn't read the side of it, didn't know if it said Millsberg or Lewisonville, but she had a sinking feeling it was the former. It was

Brody. Of course, it was. Nick had radioed Brody, and whatever numbers had come across his radio was just some secret cop code for his arrival.

She watched, feeling paralyzed, unable to move, but her eyes searched the parking lot. She took in everything—the way Nick stopped to talk to the other cop, leaning down toward the open window. He had a strong jaw, with a little dent in it. She noticed how the wind blew Nick's short, brown hair back from his angular features. Nick said something to the other cop, and then smiled. He had a nice smile. He'd seemed so nice. And appearances were so deceiving, weren't they?

She couldn't see the other officer, which was good, because she didn't want him to see her, even if it wasn't Brody. She didn't want to be seen by any more cops than necessary. She was two hours away from home, but still, the one thing she'd learned about cops, living with Brody, was that they were all brothers. And they had access to everything. They could find out anything about you they wanted to at a keyboard. Even from their cars.

Ginny found herself sinking even lower when the other cop's door swung open. She saw right away that it wasn't Brody—this cop was too fat to be Brody. Thank God. She glanced toward the door as she wrapped the rest of the donuts in napkins and put them into her backpack. Her hot chocolate was gone. It was time to go.

It wasn't until she stood, seeing the other cop in profile, that her knees went out from under her. The other cop looked like he'd spent a lot of time at Dunkin' Donuts, not necessarily drinking coffee. The other cop was as tall as Nick and, looking at the two of them together, she thought it was like looking at some strange reflection. The other cop was like an older, beefier version of his son.

You don't remember me, do you?

She remembered now.

Ginny bolted toward the bathroom, barely making it to the stall before she threw up a hot, chocolatey mess.

This isn't happening.

This can't be happening.

She stayed in the stall until Dunkin' Donuts closed, when the cashier came in to tell her. Until then, she sat on the toilet, trembling with fear. Ginny apologized to the girl, told her she was feeling ill, which wasn't a lie. She walked out on shaky legs, and found both cruisers were gone.

The video store wasn't closed yet, so she went around to the back of the building and sat under the glow of a streetlight, but she didn't take out her sketch pad. Instead, she closed her eyes and tried not to remember. She knew she should get up and take off, go somewhere far, far away, but she didn't have the energy.

How old had they been, the last time she'd seen Nick Santos? Seventh grade, maybe. That made her think of Mr. Spencer. He'd been in Mr. Spencer's math class with her, hadn't he? She thought so. That was before Nick and his dad moved from Millsberg, their tiny little town, to Lewisonville, a bustling metropolis in comparison. All ten thousand residents of it.

Why hadn't she made the connection? Maybe because it had been years since she saw them, Nick and his father. Brody still hunted with Steven Santos, she knew—it was a blissful week-long break when they went off together to drink beer and shoot at things—but she never saw the man. Steve Santos hadn't started coming around until last year—right around Christmas. And while she remembered that he had a son, she hadn't recognized Nick when she saw him.

But he had recognized her. No wonder she thought he'd been following her!

And maybe he had. Maybe he and his father were, right now, telling Brody she was holing up in Lewisonville. But she didn't think so. If Nick was going to turn her over to Brody, he would have done it already. She'd seen him for the first time at least a week ago. And they'd run into each other—literally— in the book store the other day, and he clearly recognized her, even if she hadn't recognized him.

She remembered Nick as tall, gangly, awkward and a little shy. They'd gone swimming in the summer together at the local pond. Maggie was always forced to let Ginny tag along, which her older sister resented. Ginny thought Nick had a crush on Maggie for the longest time, the way he hung around them. It was a whole summer—that was after seventh grade, she remembered—before Maggie finally told her it was Ginny he liked. But he was almost four years older, and then he moved away, and that was that.

Now here he was again. That information was enough to process, but Nick wasn't the problem, although he might turn into one. It was his father, Steven, Brody's hunting buddy, who was the real problem. And "problem" was the understatement of the century. It was Steven Santos who was the other man on the memory card sitting in her bag. He had just as much reason to find her as Brody did—and the man was right here in town.

If Nick Santos breathed one word to his father about her—even mentioned that he'd seen her—she knew she was dead. She needed a way out of this town. Out of this life. And fast. Thinking about missing Maggie and the boys on Christmas made her heart ache. She didn't want to leave them, not yet. It was only a week and a half away. Could she hide until then? Did she dare?

Could she trust Nick not to say anything?

She just didn't know.

Chapter Six

It was one in the morning when she remembered she had food in her pocket. She'd completely forgotten it in all the earlier excitement. Her stomach thanked her, making all sorts of noises as she licked powdered sugar off her fingers. It wasn't the first time hunger had woken her, that beast crawling deep in her belly, but it was one of the few times she had a little extra food.

The light outside felt different. Maybe it was just that most nights she was asleep by now, wrapped up in her coat, head on her backpack, curled tightly into the corner. She had never seen a security guard or a police car cruise the parking lot—not even Nick—but she didn't want any of her limbs hanging out in line of sight of the doorway. She had learned to be cautious. Very cautious.

When she had polished off the rest of Nick's jelly donut, she crumpled the napkin and stuck it back into her pocket. The jar of peanut butter she'd found was still there, in reserve. Sighing, she wrapped her coat around herself and curled up in the corner again.

It wasn't easy to get comfortable. The floor was hard and cold, her backpack lumpy. She tried to pack it so the clothes were on the side where she rested her head. There wasn't ever any getting away from the cold, even bundled up. Her fingers and toes were always freezing, and in the morning, they were stiff and they ached. In fact, her whole body felt that way. Still, her stomach no longer felt like it was eating itself. She was relieved that, for a little while, she might be able to get some peace, just a brief respite, a few hours of sleep. She'd think about what she was going to do tomorrow.

It came like a strange cross between a memory and a dream. Brody in his uniform wielding a broom like a nightstick, the closest thing he could find, chasing a pregnant Maggie into a corner and beating her until the handle broke. Ginny stood frozen in dream-like paralysis in the doorway, her fear overriding her guilt at not moving to defend her sister. She heard Maggie screaming and Brody yelling at her.

"Get out! Get the fuck out! Get out before the cops come!"

Ginny's head came up, fuzzy and throbbing upon waking, as if she had been the one beaten. She understood it was a dream, and realized the words, still echoing in her head, *"Get out before the cops come!"* weren't Brody's words at all. They were very real—and they were coming from inside the video store.

There were people inside the video store and they were heading toward the exit—*her exit.* She saw three of them, heads bobbing back and forth over the shelves. Ginny moved without thinking, knowing she had to get out of there. She crouched, grabbing her backpack and reaching for the door handle. They were coming now, one of them stopping to punch a security code.

"Let's get the fuck out of here, Luke! Hurry up!"

Ginny stood, ready to run. There was just no time. A few minutes earlier and she could have been safely in the alleyway behind the building. There was no avoiding it now. They saw her the minute the door swung open and everyone stood rigid, the shock of being caught leaving them all stunned and breathless.

For a moment, she thought she might faint, but she willed it not to happen.

The tall one broke the spell, hissing, "Go, man! Fucking GO! GO! GO!" They all pushed past her to the exit, knocking her aside.

Her backpack caught onto something one of them was holding. She felt a sharp tug, something gave way, and the guy bringing up the rear gave up the struggle as he continually repeated, "She saw us!" while they all fumbled out the door.

It was over as quickly as it had started. She stood for a moment, watching their tail lights disappear out of the parking lot, wondering if she had been dreaming. She looked down at her feet and saw what one of them had dropped. She hesitated only a moment before she grabbed it and bolted out the door, running in the opposite direction until the ache in her side forced her to slow.

She didn't even know where she was. She had run into the neighborhood behind the strip mall, and had made as many turns as she could, hoping no one was watching or following her. Panting, she sat down on the curb next to a parked car. Leaning her head against the bumper, she tried to stop shaking. She felt faint for a moment, but the feeling washed over her and then passed.

She couldn't live this way anymore. She had to do something. Anything. No matter where she went, she felt as if the world were closing in on her, as if she really was the trash Brody always claimed, being compacted into a neat little throwaway piece. She and Maggie had lived under the cloud of Brody's viewpoint for so long they both believed it was true—they didn't deserve any better.

But the boys did.

Ginny remembered them this afternoon, a million years ago now—Sean's sticky hand in hers, Michael's long legs flailing underneath him on the swing, begging for purchase. She was determined neither of them would ever know what it would be like to live as human garbage.

The tears came. She swiped at them, but they came too fast for her to stop them, falling onto the bag lying between her feet. Her hands trembled as she picked it up and, without thinking, she pulled the drawstring and looked inside.

"No," she whispered, feeling instant salvation and damnation settle in the pit of her stomach like an anchor.

There was no denying the reality of what was in the bag. She took it out and counted it there in the glow of a streetlight, and then she counted it again, because it was more cash than she'd ever seen in her lifetime.

Twelve-hundred dollars.

She looked around, but the street retained the early morning quiet the suburbs often did, house lights dark, blinds closed, a world asleep. Just standing was a struggle, between the exhaustion and the weight that felt as if it had been lodged somewhere beneath her rib cage. She didn't know how she was going to manage to walk to the shelter in this state.

She was no longer a part of this world where houses were warm, beds were soft, and food existed as if by magic in refrigerators. She wanted this world for the boys. It was the best Christmas gift she could think of to give them.

She tucked the money deep into her backpack and zipped it, shrugging it on, ignoring the taut ache of her muscles and the numbing exhaustion creeping into her limbs. She walked just to keep moving, unsure of her destination, following the thought of sleep like an illusion, a mirage she chased on some distant moonlit pavement.

"Hey, Mags, do you remember Nick Santos?" Ginny asked her sister as they went through the dumpster out behind the mission.

"Oh my God, what made you think of him?" Maggie brushed hair out of her face with her mittens, glancing behind her at the boys climbing up the distant hill. They were little dots from where they stood, their high voices, calling to one another and laughing, carrying toward them on the wind.

"I saw him the other day." Ginny's voice echoed in the dumpster as she hung halfway in to reach a perfect boy-sized cardboard box. She pulled it out, triumphant, tossing it next to the other one she'd found behind the dumpster. It had grease on the bottom, but that was fine, because it had a sort of wax coating all over. That's exactly what she was looking for.

"Oh yeah." Maggie frowned, her brow knitted. "Isn't his dad... oh fuck. Ginny, his dad's the chief of police here!"

Ginny nodded, taking paper out of the box and tossing it into the dumpster.

"Does he know I'm here?" Maggie shook her arm, eyes wide. "Oh God, how did I not remember that?"

"He doesn't know about you." Ginny put one box into the other. "But Nick saw me. We talked. I didn't tell him anything."

"Thank God." Maggie relaxed a little. "I can't wait to get out of here. I'm so glad Tim forgot about the money in the safety deposit box. That means we can get that apartment."

"I'm glad, too." Ginny had given her the money and told her it came from the safety deposit box. The decision hadn't been an easy one, exactly—but despite the wrongness of it, it felt like the right thing to do at the time.

More than anything, she wanted to see her sister and her nephews in their own place before Christmas, safe and happy, before she left. Once her sister was established, once she started working, Brody would find her. Brody would come looking for Ginny, come looking for the evidence she had in her bag, and Ginny would have to be gone. There was no way around that. But until then, she thought they would be safe enough.

Relatively safe. That's what she had to live with until she could get on a bus and go somewhere safer. Nick knowing her, knowing Maggie, was a problem, but she really believed, if he was going to say something, it would have happened already. Besides, Brody had seen her in the coffee shop, so he was likely looking all over Millsberg for Ginny. He didn't suspect she was here, in a neighboring town, two hours away. He knew Tim and Maggie had split, of course, but he didn't know where Maggie was. At least, she hoped not. And Tim... well, he had disappeared with all of Maggie's cash, including whatever had been in the safe deposit box, and Ginny didn't think he would ever come back.

"Gin..." Maggie stopped her as they headed toward the hill, tugging on her sleeve.

"What?" She was carrying the boxes as she turned to face her sister. Maggie looked more relaxed than she'd seen her in weeks.

"I'm sorry about the other day." Maggie's eyes started to well up with tears. "I'm just so stressed. You have no idea. It's so hard, telling the boys their dad isn't coming back... and trying to reassure them that it's all going to be okay..."

"I know." Ginny felt her own chin start to tremble, tears threatening, too. She knew about stress. She knew about trying to make it all look okay. She knew—but she couldn't say anything to her sister. She wouldn't. It was Maggie and the boys she wanted to protect, and even if it killed her, she was going to do that. "I know, Mags. I know."

Maggie reached out and hugged her, knocking the boxes out of Ginny's arms into the snow. Ginny hugged her back, feeling hot tears falling, trying to wish them away. It was almost over. She would stay through Christmas, and then she would head to California, somewhere Brody would never find her. He might talk to Maggie, he might even threaten her, if he found her, but only to try to find out where Ginny was. He didn't want to have anything to do with Maggie, anymore—not since Sean had been born. She was damaged goods.

Ginny was the one he wanted now.

"I love you, Gin," her sister whispered in her ear.

"I know," Ginny whispered back, taking what comfort she could in her sister's arms, like she used to when she skinned her knee falling off her bike. "I love you too, Mags."

It had been hard on both of them, not having a mother, Ginny realized, as they parted. Maggie helped her with the boxes, grabbing one and handing her the other as they marched toward the hill. They'd lost their mother and had lost the stepfather-lottery big time, but they'd made the best of it. It made them closer, really, in the end. But she thought Maggie had gotten the worst of it, because while Maggie was playing the mother role, she had no one around to mother her.

Now, she was a real mother, with two very real little boys she loved very much, and Ginny thought they were the luckiest little kids in the world. Her sister had always been a good mother to Ginny, and now she was a good mother to them. Ginny was glad the boys had her.

"You guys ready to go sledding?" Ginny called to her nephews. They were rolling around in the snow, giggling together.

"We don't have sleds." Sean looked askance at the boxes.

"Aunt Ginny is going to make you each a sled," Maggie told them with a smile as she handed her sister the other box. Ginny was already tearing and folding the cardboard, assessing the size of each of them as she did. "She's very resourceful."

You don't know the half of it, Ginny thought, feeling her sister's hand on her shoulder.

And, if Ginny had anything to do with it, she never would.

Chapter Seven

She had just missed the seven-day advance-purchase ticket price. It was a fifty-dollar difference that meant she didn't have enough money left over to stay somewhere like the local YWCA or even the one small youth hostel in the area. She hadn't dared to go back to the video store. Instead, she'd been sleeping in cul-de-sacs and beneath underpasses.

With the wind whipping up under her long coat, the cold was so pervasive and relentless, she shivered in a permanent state of misery. Her normal body temperature became a constant fever, leaving her teeth chattering. She longed for the relative warmth that existed between two panes of glass, a place that somehow had come to feel like home.

She had headed over to do some more research about the San Francisco Art Institute and the possibility of financial aid, but she had forgotten the library had shortened hours, now that it was getting close to Christmas. She found herself out on the street again before it was even dark, facing an hour's walk back to town.

Last night, she had slept in the recessed doorway of the high school only a few blocks away from Maggie's new place on Fourth Street, choosing a door facing away from the road. She spent most of the night awake, worrying about the possibility of being found and fantasizing about the relief of the video store's vestibule around the corner.

She knew she had been lucky with the unseasonable warmth, but she'd heard a weather report this morning that foretold temperatures tonight dropping well below freezing with the possibility of snow. This portent arrived as she trudged her way back into town, walking down a street in a small downtown area lined with fun little shops where people were taking their very last opportunity to buy gifts.

A little girl stood in front of the bakery holding some sort of cinnamon bun that made Ginny's stomach clench. The child turned to the woman next to her and cried, "Mommy, look, it's snowing!" The tone was one Ginny remembered echoing like some distant memory, that awed and giddy voice which made anything around Christmas sound magical.

Ginny looked up and saw small white flakes floating against the light of one of the lamp posts. The town's holiday decorations, a candy cane and two silver bells flocked by evergreen branches, were just starting to gather the first bit of white dust.

The little girl had her tongue out, trying to catch the larger flakes, and her mother smiled indulgently. The woman caught Ginny watching them and commented, "Perfect timing for Christmas, isn't it?" before she steered her daughter out of the way of shoppers and they made their way down the street.

What was perfect timing for everyone else's holiday felt like a warped and unjust act of God to Ginny. More snow! As she watched the mother and daughter pair retreat, something heavy settled in her belly, a pain that went deeper than hunger.

Her indecision stopped her at the intersection. Where was she going to spend the night? She glanced back at the street scene—traffic crawling, cars looking for places to park, people milling between stores, gloved hands clutching packages or bags. It reminded her of a snow globe she had as a kid, one of those cheap plastic things you shook in order to watch the snow fall on a city street.

She smiled at the memory. Maggie had given her that funny little globe, the one that looked so odd and stilted with all the snow gathered in clumps on the bottom. Still, in those few seconds when everything turned upside down and then righted again, when those unidentifiable little white pellets floated through liquid in a sweet simulation of snow falling, everything seemed right with the world. Ginny found herself feeling homesick.

Maggie had asked her to come hang out with them, even spend the night, but she had refused. She knew if she spent even one night with them, she would never want to leave. It would just sap her courage and urgency to get on the bus when it was time to go.

That wasn't the only reason, of course. The main reason was she still worried about being followed, and she didn't want to lead Brody anywhere near Maggie's new place. Putting herself in danger was one thing, but putting them all at risk was something else altogether.

The decision weighed heavily on her as she stood on the street corner and watched the snow fall. She knew if she went left, she wouldn't end up at the high school but rather on her sister's doorstep. She just couldn't do that. Eyeing the coffee house across the street to her right, she knew it closed late. She could kill some time and it would allow her to sketch for a while. Just down the street from the cafe, she was drawn to the promise of a warm, safe night tucked in the vestibule at the video store.

If she couldn't have the nestled calm of Maggie's home, the video store felt like the next best thing. It had been a week since the robbery and the memory of it seemed distant compared to the ache she was feeling for something, anything, familiar. She made her decision, turning right, noticing enough snow had already fallen for her to leave footprints behind her as she headed to the coffee house.

With great relief, she settled into her spot on the floor of the vestibule. Fatigue crept into her joints and bones as the warmth began to thaw her limbs. She stretched out onto her back and watched the snow falling, more heavily now. Her bus ticket was tucked away in her pocket, and although she dreamed about warm beaches and sunshine, she felt a bit sad that this might be the last snowfall she saw for a very long time.

It seemed impossible that spending the night alone and homeless, watching it snow from the entrance of a video store, was preferable to the night spent at the place she had always known as home. But the closer it got to Christmas, when she thought of this time last year, she knew she had a lot to be grateful for tonight.

When Brody had dragged her from her bed in the middle of the night, she found herself looking up through the branches of the little tabletop tree she had decorated in an attempt to create some semblance of a normal Christmas. She wondered how she ever could have believed in something as benevolent as Santa Claus. She was getting the only gift she would get from her stepfather that year, as he knelt between her legs while his cop friend and hunting buddy, Steve Santos, forced himself into her mouth.

Merry fucking Christmas, sweetheart.

There was the hope, now she had escaped, her life could unfold, and she clung to that. The envelope in her pocket was the ticket to a freedom she could only begin to imagine. She felt a greater anticipation tonight than she had ever felt before, her whole body tingling with it as she watched the magic of the snow falling down, remembering the snow globe and how you had to turn the world upside down to make it snow.

Her whole world had turned upside down, but all was right somehow. She felt something filling her, something she very seldom felt, a novel belief that something good was coming. Perhaps it was just the promise of the holiday, the weighted expectation of Christmas coming. Her blood sang with it every year, and it was operatic now, filled with something beyond the feeling she had when she was young and thought she might glimpse Santa leaving something in their stockings.

Somehow, she was surprised, but no more shocked that night than she was the year before, when a door opened, and the safety of her universe collapsed under the weight of a man. There were two of them and she recognized the tall one right away, the one who had punched in the security code. The other had a jacket she recognized, black with blue stripes.

Her quick instincts might have saved her if it hadn't been for the length of her own coat. She was up and had the door open before they were on her, but one of them stepped on the hem and she was brought up short. It was just long enough for him to grab her by the arm and twist her back into the vestibule, pressing her hard against the glass. It was the tall one. She could see his reflection, although her breath was beginning to fog it enough for it to be unclear.

"Where's our fucking money, bitch?" He pulled her toward him only to shove her back hard, her cheek pressed against the cold surface of the glass. She gasped but didn't say anything—she knew it wouldn't matter.

"Look through her bag, idiot," he urged his friend in the blue/black coat, who then yanked it off her shoulder. She saw his reflection pulling out clothes, her sketchpad, her toiletries, tossing them aside.

"Nothing," blue/black coat said, tossing her bag into the corner. "Hold her."

Ginny closed her eyes against his hands digging into her coat pockets, pulling out a bus ticket, twenty dollars in cash, and a Scrunchie.

"Well, she spent some of it on this." Blue/black coat showed the tall one her bus ticket, then shoved it, and the cash, into his pocket.

"You gonna skip town with our money? Where is it?" The tall one twisted her arm tighter.

Ginny felt herself leaving, floating somewhere above them, gone, nowhere near her body in that moment. She couldn't have answered him if she wanted to. She knew it was only a matter of time, and she was right.

The tall one spun her around, snatching her coat off and throwing it over her bag. "Maybe she's got it hidden somewhere under all this."

Their hands were on her, pulling, pushing, leaving her cold and trembling, stripping her down. The floating, observant part of her was amused at their frustration with all her extra layers of clothing.

"Told you she wouldn't still have it." Blue/black coat eyed her shivering form in jeans and t-shirt.

"Haven't checked everywhere." The tall one grunted as he unzipped and tried to shove her jeans down her hips over her leggings. "Come on, help me."

Blue/black coat took over the tugging, and their hands were on her, searching, probing. It was when the tall one turned her around and pressed her into the glass again and blue/black coat pulled her leggings down to her knees, that the disembodied part of herself came home.

Finally finding her voice, she flailed and screamed at them.

The tall one clamped his hand over her mouth, using his other arm across her midsection to pull her in tight against him, crushing the air out of her.

"You better shut up," he warned.

Feeling him pressed against her behind, she knew what it was and what he intended to do with it. She was still screaming, but nothing came out. She bit down hard on his hand and he swore, shoving her head hard enough against the glass it created a small spider web crack. Seeing blackness, then stars in the blackness, it was only then she felt the pain exploding through her head like white-hot fireworks.

Moaning, she heard one of them say something about getting her, teaching her. Her ears were ringing, her head on fire. There was more tugging, ripping, her panties gone, then she was being bent over. Her voice resurfaced, and she found herself screaming again.

"Shut her up!" blue/black coat hissed, then someone hit her hard across the mouth and she tasted blood.

Still, she couldn't stop screaming, and the hand came again, this time in the form of a fist. It felt as if something in her head rattled loose with that hit and the voice stopped. Everything stopped. Sound receded. Light faded. She sank quickly, falling, dying, and all she felt was a final relief, an overwhelming sense of gratitude.

"The cops!" Blue/black coat yelled and the tall one dropped her.

She crumpled to her knees.

They bolted out the opposite door into the snow, but she didn't see them, just heard them. She dry heaved onto the floor—there was nothing in her stomach to come up, but she convulsed as if there were.

She became aware of boots, a familiar blue uniform. Large hands held her hair back as she trembled and heaved, murmuring something unintelligible. She turned her head to look and her heart sank when she saw him, the same man she'd seen in the library, at Barnes and Noble, in the 7-Eleven and Dunkin' Donuts, the one who had a crush on her back when they were kids.

"Nick," she croaked before slipping into a blissful, empty and painless darkness.

Chapter Eight

She woke up floating on a cloud. Her body ached but she rested on something so soft it was unimaginable. Her eyes focused and she realized she was in someone's home. She was on a sofa and there was a television, a coffee table, all the usual living room amenities, along with a Christmas tree in the corner. One stocking hung on the fireplace mantle. She heard someone talking and, for a moment, couldn't remember anything that had happened.

He was on the phone. She sat bolt upright, suddenly remembering everything.

Nick was on the phone. Who was he talking to? Who was he telling?

Scanning the room for her backpack and coat, she found them in a corner. The world slipped a little as she stood. Steadying herself on the arm of a chair, she moved toward her things. She had to get out before Brody showed up.

Nick moved further into the kitchen, his voice muffled. She strained to hear. Was he calling more cops? Worse, was he calling Brody? She shivered, sure it was the latter as she shrugged on her coat and shouldered her backpack, easing toward the front door.

"Hey! Hey there! Hold on!"

She heard him call out as she turned the knob. She pulled, but found the deadbolt locked.

He caught up to her in three quick strides, and as she unlocked the deadbolt and pulled open the door, he pressed his hand flat against it and shut it again.

"Where do you think you're going?"

"Anywhere but here!" She moved around him, starting toward the kitchen.

"Listen, you have to stay." He caught up again, moving in front of her to block the entryway with his body.

"Like hell I do!" She shoved at him, but it was like trying to move a brick wall, and her head and mouth throbbed with the effort. "What for? So, you and Brody can finish what those two started? I don't think so, asshole! Now get out of my way!"

"Brody? Your stepdad? What are you talking about?" The genuine look of confusion on his face stopped her for a moment.

"Do they give you acting lessons in private dick school?" she snarled, turning away from him and running toward the front door.

"We can't keep doing this running thing all night." Exasperated, he caught up with her again, stepping in front of the door before she could reach it.

"Then get out of my way."

"What are you running from? What are you running to?"

She swallowed hard, throat burning, voice shaking.

"If you had any idea what I was running from, you never would've told him where I am. Now get out of my way!" She ducked under his arm, pulling at the door, but was no match for the weight of him pressed against it.

"Listen to me!" He grabbed her arms and pulled her toward him. "I'm trying to help you. That's all I want to do!"

"If you want to help, then let me go," she pleaded. "Please, whatever he's told you, none of it is true. You can't let him find me. I'm *begging* you."

The tears were coming, and she couldn't stop them, although she tried hard. She even bit down on her bruised and swollen lip, hoping the pain might be a distraction.

"What are you talking about?" He shook his head at her.

"Oh, come on, you know who! The guy you were just talking to on the phone!" She pulled away from him and ran—she didn't care anymore where to.

This time when he reached her, he enfolded her, wrapping his arms around her from behind, grabbing her wrists and crossing them over. He held her that way for some time, not speaking, just waiting for her to stop struggling. When her breath began to slow a little and she relaxed against his bulk, he finally spoke.

"I'm going to tell you something and I want you to listen. Then I'm going to ask you a question and you're going to answer me. Do you understand?"

He waited for her to nod, which she did reluctantly, before going on.

"I wasn't on the phone with Brody," he assured her. "I haven't told anyone anything, Ginny. That was my partner on the phone. I told her I wasn't coming into work tomorrow, that's all."

She relaxed a little at these words, not sure what to believe.

"Look, I know you've been sleeping at the video store for the past few weeks."

She let that information sink in, not knowing if she could or should trust what he was saying.

"Now... is Brody looking for you? Did you run away?"

"You... really don't know?" she asked, her voice small. She felt him sigh.

"I don't know much. I know what I think. I think you ran away and you clearly have nowhere to go. You're obviously very afraid of something... or someone... sounds like you and Brody had some kind of falling out? And you seemed to like the peanut butter and apple juice I left out for you."

She gasped, flushing, and she knew what he was saying had to be true. It all came at her, everything, the weeks alone, the terror of believing Brody was looking for her, having her followed, the harsh words and hard hands. It came with so much force she gasped and then sobbed, collapsing as if she was a puppet and someone had just cut her strings.

He gathered her up and sat with her on the sofa. She found herself clinging to him, desperate for someone who might be able to offer even just a little comfort.

"What happened?" he asked her again, and she found herself telling him, in small bursts, about her stepfather and his abuse.

"So, you ran away?" He stroked her hair and she found herself sinking against him, nodding. "And you thought he called me about you?"

She nodded again, closing her eyes, feeling more comfortable here in Nick's arms than she had anywhere in a very long time.

He took a deep breath, and then he said something she had never heard a man say in her life. "Well, you're safe now. I won't let anyone hurt you."

"Thank you." She put her arms around him, feeling a warmth and easiness that should have taken years to accomplish, given her justifiable tendency toward mistrust.

"I'm so sorry that happened to you, Ginny." He sighed again, hand still in her hair. "But you know..."

He leaned back to look at her, and she saw something in his eyes that stopped her, some internal struggle that put her on edge.

"What?" she asked.

He cleared his throat.

"We really should make a report."

He said it as if he knew what her response would be. She leapt out of his lap, practically hissing.

"Okay, okay," he conceded, encircling her wrists with his hands and pulling her back toward him. "I'll tell you what. You stay here tonight."

She looked down at him, suspicious.

"You can have a bath and I'll make you something to eat," he said, tempting her, but she was far too skeptical to give in. He looked at her like he could read her mind, saying, "Don't worry, I have a guest room. Then tomorrow, we'll talk about more about this, okay?"

"Brody's a cop," she reminded him. "The minute my name is in any system, I'm dead."

He nodded sympathetically.

"They took my bus ticket to California and the only money I had to my name." She sank into the chair opposite him, the realization finally hitting her. All her dreams of California and art school had vanished in one five-minute struggle. "I don't know what I'm going to do."

"It's going to be okay," he assured her, his hand swallowing hers as he helped her to stand.

For some reason beyond her comprehension, looking into his quiet, dark eyes, she believed him.

After weeks of bathing in a bathroom sink, Ginny moaned out loud when she slid into a full, hot tub of water. Nick had insisted on the compromise of taking digital pictures of her face on his iPhone before he gave her towels and let her into the bathroom. She didn't know how long she spent soaking after she'd washed everything three times, including her hair. She may have even slept a little in the heat, startling out of her daze when he knocked.

"Hey, food's ready," he called through the door.

"Give me just a minute." She reached for a towel.

"If you want, leave your clothes and I'll throw them in the machine," he told her. "There's a shirt on the door that should cover you. Come down when you're ready."

"Okay." She pulled the plug and let the bath water drain.

Wrapped in a towel, she inspected her face. Her lip was swollen and blue on one side, and she had a bruise already on the same side of her cheek that looked as if it might grow darker. The lump on the left side of her forehead hurt the most. It was the size of a quarter, red in the center and purple at the edges.

She towel-dried her hair and found the white button-down shirt he'd left hanging on the door. It was enormous and came to her knees. She debated about a bra and panties or leggings for a moment, and decided to let him wash everything and just wear the shirt.

"Nick?" She found him setting the table in the kitchen.

He was still in his uniform and just looking at him in it brought a tangled combination of feeling—apprehension and security. She smiled at him anyway.

"I'm starving!"

He stood frozen, forks and napkins halted in midair, looking at her wearing his shirt and standing framed by the doorway. Ginny glanced down and noticed her still-wet hair leaving little see-through patches on the material in places. She saw the lustful look in his eyes. It made her flush and felt a low heat burning below the hunger in her belly.

"What'd you make?" She decided to brazen it out and walked toward him, where he still stood, as if transfixed. She cocked her head at him and met his gaze. There was more than kindness in them now, she noticed, although he looked quickly away, as if he wanted to hide his feelings.

Clearing his throat, he managed to answer, "Spaghetti. Have a seat."

She did, her stomach growling at the smell and thought of food. She'd discovered hunger was interesting in that way. There were times when the stomach seemed to forget for a while that it hadn't been satisfied, but the sight or smell of something could bring that instant gnarl and clench again.

She was ravenous and devoured it all, an entire plate of pasta and sauce, her own roll with butter and half of his. He watched her as he chewed thoughtfully. She thought he looked preoccupied with something, but she was so engrossed in satisfying her own senses she didn't care.

It was only when her belly was full that thoughts began again, and she asked him, "So... you live alone here?"

His smile was strained, and she didn't realize until that moment how callous her question might have been. But she'd seen pictures on the mantle—him and some girl. They looked happy together. There were even pictures of him with Nick's family—well, Nick's dad. Seeing that had stopped her cold.

"I moved in here with... someone... but it didn't work out." He shrugged.

"What about your dad? Do you have anything for dessert?" She ran the two questions together and he laughed. "Did you tell your dad about me?"

"No, I didn't tell anyone," he said, standing. "I have some Ben and Jerry's I think. Want me to check?"

She nodded, contemplating this information. "Did your father ask about me?"

"Why would he?" he asked, head in the freezer.

"No cops, okay?" She looked at him in earnest. "Please. No cops. Just you. No one else."

"Okay." He held up two containers. "Do you want Chunky Monkey or Phish Food?"

"Oh, yes!" She smiled. "Both!"

"Brody *is* looking for you." He gave her this piece of information slowly. "A missing person's report was filed. It came across my desk last week."

"I figured." She met his eyes, trying to tell if he was really being honest with her. "Nick, you have to tell me the truth. I know Brody and your dad are friends..."

The memory of this man's father was far too close, his beefy, groping hands. But she couldn't tell him the truth. She couldn't possibly.

"He doesn't know you're here." Nick shook his head. "I promise."

"Please don't tell anyone." She tried not to sound like she was begging, but it still came out as a plea as she watched him take down two bowls and pull out spoons. "Not anyone."

"Ginny, why did you run away?" he asked as she started clearing the table, taking their dishes to the sink while he scooped the ice cream.

"I'm eighteen. I'm not a runaway." She put her chin out, feeling defiant.

"You know what I mean," he replied softly, turning her face toward him so she had to meet his eyes.

"He... hurt me." She swallowed, feeling the tremble in her mouth. "Just... leave it at that."

Nick nodded slowly, handing over her ice cream without another word.

They settled on the sofa with their bowls and Ginny let each bite of cold, creamy sweetness melt in her mouth, eyes closing in relief. She hadn't been warm and fed like this in a while. He watched her with a very similar expression on his face.

"Nice TV." She nodded toward the big screen, trying to make conversation.

"Yeah, it was her idea to buy it," he admitted with a shrug, finding the remote and flicking it on. Ginny realized he'd mistaken her comment as a hint. "But I don't use it much. Not a lot of time to watch really..."

"Hey, *It's a Wonderful Life!*" she exclaimed through a mouthful of ice cream.

"I'm beginning to think it might be." Nick smiled, his gaze lingering on her mouth where she licked a bit of chocolate off her lower lip.

"Don't you love this movie?" She felt his gaze on her like a heat and turned her attention to the screen instead. Her skin tingled, as if his gaze had touched her flesh. "I haven't seen it in years. When I was little, somehow it never felt like Christmas unless I saw it at least once."

"It's a classic," he agreed. "My mom and I used to watch it every year."

"Mine, too." Ginny sucked thoughtfully on her spoon as the opening credits began to run.

"Well, then, let's you and me do the holidays right for a change," he said, standing up with conviction. "Who wants popcorn?"

"With butter?" Ginny's eyes brightened.

"At least a stick," he replied with a grin. "Cholesterol and triglycerides be damned!"

He was in the kitchen before she could say a word. Despite her reservations and the strange, even surreal, unfolding events of the night, she found herself more comfortable here than she had been in a long time—perhaps ever.

The movie was just starting, the familiar music opening a floodgate. It brought back instant memories of Christmases when she and Maggie, as very young girls, had snuggled together against their mother as they watched the old angel try to get his wings. It was one of her earliest memories.

That was before Brody.

She was lost in her memories, drifting, her eyes even closing a little as she listened to the lull of popcorn popping in the kitchen. It was the smell of it wafting into the room that made her lift her head to see Nick coming back with a huge bowl. He set it between them on the couch. Ginny let her fingers slip into the fluffy, buttery fluff, bringing some to her mouth. Nick watched her, looking pleased.

"Thank you," she murmured after a moment, glancing over at him.

"Popcorn's easy," he replied with a shrug, his hand brushing hers in the bowl.

"No... not the popcorn." Ginny nudged him with her elbow.

"You're welcome. Now, eat! My mother would turn over in her grave if I didn't live up to my heritage someday by using that phrase. Am I right?"

She laughed, curling her feet under her and digging into the bowl. The movie was long, and they didn't talk much, but their hands brushed every now and then, when they reached for more buttery goodness. Ginny found herself drifting again, lost in her memories of childhood Christmases.

"She's happy with so little," Nick murmured, startling her out of her reverie.

"Who?" She looked thoughtfully at Donna Reed welcoming Jimmy Stewart "home" to a broken-down old house on their wedding night.

"I don't know." He shook his head. "I guess I'm just so used to dating women who want the big house and the expensive car and everything else that goes with it. It's not who a guy is, anymore—it's what he does, and more importantly, how much money he makes doing it."

"No," she replied, meeting his gaze. "All of that... it's just stuff. Sure, it's nice, but it's really not what matters."

He leaned his head back on the couch, eyes searching her face. "You're really something, you know that?"

She shrugged. "I'm nothing special."

"No, you're wrong." His voice changed, growing firmer. "And I wish more people in your life had told you so."

"I've got enough people in my life telling me I'm wrong, thank you very much."

He smiled, reaching out to touch her bruised cheek, rubbing it gently with his thumb. "You know what I mean."

She glanced from him to the screen. His eyes were soft when they met hers, questioning even. They made her feel warm all over. He turned slightly toward her, and the light of the television glinted off his badge. Her eyes lingered there, then moved up to his face again. With her associations, it was hard for her to reconcile the two. Yet here he was, wearing the same uniform and yet so very different from Brody. So different from his own father.

"The thing about her is..." Ginny's gaze flicked from him to the television. "She knows a good thing when she sees it."

"You think so?" His thumb moved over her jaw.

"Yes," she insisted, although her eyes were on him now, not on the couple on the screen. "There aren't many men who would offer a girl the moon."

Nick surprised her by doing a Jimmy Stewart impression, stutter and all. "What is it you want, Mary? What do you want? You want the moon? Just say the word and I'll throw a lasso around it and pull it down."

"I'll take it," Ginny quoted, smiling at him.

"I wish I could give it to you."

She held her breath as he leaned forward, brushing the hair away from her face so his lips could touch her forehead. Everything inside of her went silent.

"You're very sweet." She wasn't surprised to hear her voice trembling and slightly hoarse.

"Are you done with this?" he asked, breaking the mood and nodding at the popcorn bowl. He set it aside when she didn't reply. Putting his arm across the back of the couch behind her, he settled back again to watch the movie.

By the time George Bailey was delivering his own line about moons and lassos, Nick's arm was around her shoulder, and Ginny's head was resting against his chest. It seemed natural and easy.

She didn't know if it was the amount of food her body wasn't used to digesting, or just the overwhelming weariness, but she found herself relaxed enough to even start drifting off to sleep in his arms.

"Come on," he said, nudging her.

"But Clarence hasn't gotten his wings yet..." She protested, blinking at the screen.

"I'm sorry, but you aren't going to make it, angel." He smiled.

Her body knew he was right and she followed him, already anticipating the extravagant comfort of a bed for the first time in weeks. It was a full-sized bed, nothing fancy, plain white sheets and a plaid comforter—a man's decorating taste.

He pulled the covers down for her. "You know where the bathroom is right? My room is past the bathroom at the end of the hall if you need anything. Okay?"

She nodded, her body slipping between the sheets, and she sighed and moaned at the luxurious pleasure of it. Her eyes closed of their own volition, and she whispered, "Thank you, oh, thank you," as he turned off the light.

He stepped out and started to close the door, but the impending darkness made her open her eyes again.

"Nick?" she called, voice plaintive.

"Yes?" He peeked back in.

She couldn't form the words, but she wanted to.

Instead, she just whispered, "Goodnight."

"Goodnight, angel."

In spite of her hesitation, she drifted off to sleep before the door clicked closed.

Chapter Nine

"Ginny?" Nick, whispering. "Are you okay?"

"Yeah," she whispered back, head coming up off the pillow, disoriented.

"You were crying. Are you sure?"

"I was?" She put her hands to her cheeks. They were damp. "I'm sorry, I didn't mean to wake you."

"I just wanted to make sure you're okay..."

"I guess." She drew a shaky breath and stared up at the ceiling. "Yeah... I'm okay."

"Well... goodnight then." Nick went to close the door.

"Wait." She found the light spilling in from the hallway inviting and his presence comforting. He stood, waiting.

"Would you...?" She took a deep breath. "Could you sit with me... until I fall asleep?

"Sure."

He moved back into the room, pulling a soft chair from the corner up next to the bed as she settled back down under the covers. The sound of his breathing was comforting, and she noticed how his bulk filled the chair, how he filled out his uniform, so unlike Brody's wiry frame. Thinking about Brody and the events of the night made her restless again.

"Nick," she whispered, looking to see if he was asleep.

"Hm?"

"I should tell you something." She didn't know why she said it but there it was. He didn't respond, just waited, his breathing deep and even in the darkness. "I have something that Brody wants."

"What's that?" Nick asked when she didn't continue.

"It's an SD memory card. It has a video on it." Her hand instinctively reached for the bag next to the bed that was never more than an arm's reach away. She felt his silence, waiting for her to go on.

"I was doing a project," she explained. She wouldn't tell him everything. Not everything. She wouldn't tell him that his father was on the tape too. "It was this multimedia thing for art class. I borrowed a video camera from my teacher and I was going to do this whole... never mind, that part doesn't matter..." She took a deep breath, remembering her own discovery that night. "Brody and a bunch of his friends showed up and kicked me out. I just left the tape running. He... he gets mad when I don't do what he wants, like, right away..."

"What did you see when you looked at the tape?" Nick exhaled slowly in the darkness.

"One of the guys was a dealer," she whispered, closing her eyes, the darkness giving her more courage to tell him.

"Go on."

"They argued. There was a fight." The silence stretched, and she knew she had to tell him now. "And... Brody killed him."

"You have that on tape?" Nick asked, the soft tone of his voice never changing.

"There was a knife... in Brody's hand... and the blood... so much blood..." She shivered at the memory. That wasn't everything, though. That wasn't all the camera had captured.

"He knows you have it?"

"I told him," she admitted, face burning at the memory. "The day I left, I told him if he came after me, I'd take it to some news station..."

"Jesus. I'm surprised he didn't kill you, too." Nick let out a low whistle.

"I ran." She curled up under the covers.

"I'm glad he didn't catch you."

"Me, too," she sighed. "Anyway, I just thought you should know..."

"Thank you for telling me."

It grew quiet again and she tossed and turned on the bed, wondering what he was thinking.

"Ginny, I need you to give me that SD memory card."

"No!" Her eyes grew wide at the thought.

"I understand you're scared," he went on. "But what Brody did..."

"You don't understand," she insisted, sitting and pulling the covers up to her chin. "You can't give that tape to the cops! Brody *is* a cop!"

"I know," he said, his voice soft, soothing. "But not all cops are like him. You can trust me, Ginny. I won't give it to the wrong people. I'll give it to someone who will use it to punish him to the fullest extent of the law. I promise you. Will you trust me?"

"No!" She drew a shaky breath, burrowing back under the covers again. "I don't know."

"It's okay. Let's talk about it in the morning."

Despite her fear of handing over the SD card, she felt like a weight had been lifted off her chest. Telling Nick had been a huge relief, even if she only told him some of the truth.

She remembered opening her eyes a few times, seeing him sitting there in the semi-darkness, hearing his breathing become deeper. She wondered if he was falling asleep too. Finally, she sank deep enough her whole body relaxed in ways she could barely remember.

She was cold. Shivering. He had found her hiding place and she was running from him, barefoot in the snow. She gasped herself awake in the semi-darkness, not remembering where she was. When she saw his uniformed figure standing over her, she pedaled backwards on the bed, clutching the headboard as if she could escape from him behind it. He was coming for her, and she knew only how to scream.

"Shhhhhh, Ginny, it's okay. It's me. It's Nick. You're dreaming," he murmured, trying to unclench her hands, attempting to hold her.

She struck out, twisting in his arms, panicked and kicking.

"Hey! Hey!" His voice was firm, and he shook her at the shoulders.

Her glassy eyes could only see the silver glint of his badge in the darkness. She tore at him, saying the useless words, "No, no, no!" He was much bigger than she was, much stronger, and as always, there was nothing she could do. He pinned her, for both their sakes, pressing her hands above her head and holding them at the wrists.

"Ginny! It's me. It's Nick!"

She saw him then and sobbed. "The uniform. Nick, take it off!"

He pulled back, quizzical, then she saw the dawning compassion in his eyes. He sat back on the bed, unbuttoning his uniform shirt and tossing it over a chair, badge and all.

"Better?"

She nodded, her lower lip still trembling.

"It's okay," he assured her, holding his arms out. "Do you want to come here?"

Hesitating, she looked at him, then over at the uniform resting on the chair. Just like Brody's, and yet... she knew this wasn't the same man.

"I won't hurt you," he said, as if sensing her conflict. "I just want to hold you. Comfort you."

"I'm so tired," she whispered, feeling tears welling again. She *was* tired—tired of running, tired of Brody winning. Mostly, she was tired of being so afraid all the time. Nick touched her hair, brushing it out of her face, his touch soft and gentle.

"You can rest," he murmured. "You're safe. I'm here."

Never had a man, especially one wearing that uniform, made her feel safe, but she realized he did. She could trust him, and if she let her own intuition guide her, instead of her fear, she knew it was true. Denying that was just like letting Brody win again and she was determined not to let that happen anymore.

"Hold me." She found her way to him across the bed, curling into his lap and shivering there.

He did, close, closer, trying to enfold her as she trembled against him.

"Take this off," she insisted, tugging at his belt. He looked startled for a moment, but complied, letting his uniform pants join his shirt on the chair.

She burrowed against him as if desperate for warmth, desperate for something, and he sat on the bed, holding her in his lap.

"Don't let go." Her cheek pressed against his shoulder and she straddled him, wrapping herself around him as much as she could.

"No." He made a small noise in his throat when she squeezed her legs around him.

Her tears made fast, salty trails down her cheeks, stinging her split and swollen lip. He cupped her face in his hands and kissed down the wet pathway to the corner of her mouth, and she sensed him watching for a response from her. She felt something give inside of her at his gentle urgency, a heart-rending rift along an undiscovered fault line. She half-moaned, half-sobbed, turning her mouth fully into his, tasting her own tears and blood, feeling ripped open and raw.

And she kissed him back. Her body gave her no choice.

His hand went behind her neck, his fist in her hair pulling her head sideways, slanting her mouth across his at a delicious angle as his other hand slid up her thigh, over her hip, and around her bottom, pressing her more exactly against his crotch. She gasped, feeling the throbbing hardness there, separated from her heat by only a pair of boxers and the tail ends of the shirt she wore. She couldn't help rocking against him, her mouth leaving and finding his again with every movement, forward and back, her eyes closed tight. His large hands cupped her bottom now, moving her, guiding her slow grinding hips. His tongue was trailing down her neck, making her gasp and sigh. She tilted to give him better access.

He slowed a little and she opened her eyes to meet his in the dimness, seeing a question there. He opened his mouth to speak, but she pressed her hand against his lips, murmuring the words, "Yes, yes," as she feathered kisses over his jaw and neck.

He groaned, rolling her onto her back on the bed, his hands seeking her soft, warm places under the long shirt she was wearing. She was greedy, squirming underneath him as he fumbled with her shirt, tugging at his boxers and, frustrated by the elastic, she simply slipped in through the front, finding him hard and throbbing.

He growled, her tiny hand and jerky movements under the material making him thrust against her. He tore at the front of her shirt, not hesitating to pop the last three buttons in his haste. She took the weight of him, wrapping her legs around him.

She clung to him as if she couldn't get enough, as if there would never be enough, and he let her. He left wet trails with his mouth and tongue over the swell of her breasts, grazing her hardening pink nipples with his teeth, making her shudder beneath him. His mouth moved down her belly while his hands kneaded her breasts, rolling the nipples in his fingers as he eased lower between her legs. She whimpered, his breath warm on her thighs.

"Wet!" He sounded delighted. Nick slipped a finger between her lips, then spread her open with his thumb and forefinger to expose her soft, pink folds.

She moaned as his mouth covered her flesh, his tongue flat and moving slowly back and forth. It was like flying, her body was gliding, and she could only go along for the ride, his tongue moving in ways that shifted the currents, guiding her in higher, tighter spirals. She was dizzy with the sensation, and she raked her nails over his shoulders and through his hair. He groaned against her clit when she did, and that sent an immediate jolt straight up her spine.

"Nick, please," she begged, sliding her nails down his biceps, over his forearms. "I want you. Please. I want you." Her hands were urgent, tugging, pulling at him. His face was wet with her as he kissed her thighs, her belly.

"Hungry little thing." He gave in to her desperation, sliding one knee between hers, seeking her mouth. She could taste herself on his tongue.

"Yes." She tugged at the last vestige of fabric between them. "Starving." He helped her slide his boxers down his hips and thighs. "I want you to fill me."

"I will," he promised, sliding his hand back down to her mound, grinding his palm there, his fingers playing hide and seek just at the opening of her wet little hole.

She moaned, thrusting upwards, aching for more. He slid his cock against her, rubbing it through wet folds and she moaned, opening her thighs wider and looking up at him with a hopeful expression on her face. He seemed to be re-thinking things, and he moved onto his back, pulling her on top of him. She kissed him, eager and warm and full of craving, reaching behind her to grasp his shaft, already wet from the brief but slippery run through her slit.

Her hand moved on him, and her nipples grazed his chest as she rocked. Her eyes locked with his and seemed to push his desire toward her own ravenousness. He put his hands behind his head, looking up at her, his eyes dark with lust.

"It's all yours, Ginny. Take it."

Her eyes widened, and she cocked her head to one side for a moment, hesitant. He closed his eyes and waited. She straddled him, in a full squat, watching the pulse and throb of him between her legs.

"Ohhh... oh, oh," she cried out as she rubbed the tip of him against her clit.

His eyes were still closed, but his breath was coming a little faster, his eyelids fluttering. She sank to her knees, and then slid him, slowly, past her swollen lips and into her flesh, feeling the length of him filling her, until the tip of his cock seemed to pulse at the very center of her. He let out a slow breath, his eyes half opening to see her sitting up proudly on him, and he smiled.

Her movements were hesitant at first, and then they became a slow and easy exploration of sensation, moving first right, then left, forward, back, feeling the shift of him inside her depths. He didn't touch her, just watched her moving on him, his eyes studying her face as she discovered her own rhythm. She soon began rocking keenly, her appetite deepening, her yearning growing fierce and wild as she rode him. His hands found her then, one on her hip to steady her, the other sliding a thumb between her lips to strum her clit, making her moan and throw her head back in complete abandon.

"Yessss, good," he encouraged her when she cupped her breasts in her hands, her fingers rubbing lightly over her nipples.

Her eyes were half-closed, and she could only make out the shadow of him beneath her. He was thrusting up into her now and she slowed her own movements, letting him rock her, knead and press and mold her, his easy rhythm slowly flooding her with feeling. "Don't stop."

"No," he agreed, and she felt that easy, pleasant, mellow feeling located somewhere in her belly begin to swell deliciously as he pressed deeply into her, his thumb moving in faster and faster circles on her clit. "Are you ready, sweetheart?"

She gasped, nodded, and closed her eyes. His fingers pinched her nipples hard now as those sweet waves of pleasure began to roll, fluttering pulses that seemed to pull him deeper inside of her and then unfurl outward through her limbs, leaving her floating, drifting, flying.

She collapsed onto him, shivering at the touch of his hands moving lightly up and down her back, tasting joyful tears mixed with the coppery taste of her torn lip. She couldn't stop herself from weeping, feeling overwhelmed, the well-traveled pathways of her usual neural networks completely dark, new ones opening up like lightning flashes, jolting her alive.

He wiped at her tears, kissing her wet face. "This is where we started, I think." He chuckled.

His soft kisses grew passionate, his gentle hands pressing her body more firmly against him, and she could feel him, still fully aroused inside of her. She sat up, wiping at her tears, and his hands roamed the front of her, pushing the golden curtains of her hair aside to reveal her breasts. He groaned when she slid him out of her, the wet heat of him enormous in her hand, and groaned again as she made her way down his body.

"Your mouth," he murmured, concern in his voice. He reached his fingers out to brush over bruises, but she waved him away, wanting this, even if it made her sore.

She kissed the tip of him, her tongue sliding over the head, tasting her own sticky wetness. She looked up, her eyes searching for his as her mouth slid along his length. His hands went to her hair in response, guiding her, pressing himself into her deeply, seeming to ask her to take him fully, and she did, wanting more. She gagged a little and she felt him ease up, but she pressed down again, feeling the responding thrust of him into her mouth, short little strokes that rubbed the tip against the back of her throat.

She moaned around his cock, sliding her hand down to touch herself and using her other hand to pull his skin taut, grazing up the underside of his shaft and then tickling her tongue around the ridges and edges. Ginny delighted in the hardness and softness all at once.

She explored him, feathering little kisses at the tip, tasting his pre-cum and rubbing it over her lips, moving them back down the underside, leaving a sweet, sticky trail. She enjoyed the feel, and sight of him, looking up the length of his cock and seeing it glistening and beginning to spill over as she licked his balls.

Her mouth found him again, unable to resist the throb and swell of him, slick with her juices and saliva and his own pre-cum now. He was grunting a little with every thrust into her throat, and she moaned with lust, the feel of him moving in her mouth making her hungry, even eager.

They did this dance for a long time, how long she didn't know, time seemed to disappear altogether. It was long enough that her mouth was aching and sore and her fingers, buried between her swollen pussy lips, were prunish from the wetness. He stopped her occasionally, breathing hard and urging her down to stillness until his pubic hair tickled her nose before releasing her to suck him anew.

"Ahh, Ginny, God... I need you," he said, his voice rough and harsh.

She eased her mouth off him, blowing on the shaft and then the tip, from warmth to coolness, teasing him. He growled as he moved to pull her up. Nick rolled her underneath him and searched her wetness for entry. It was found first with his fingers, then with his cock.

She gripped him, pitched into bliss, riding his fierce, driving momentum, and she found herself skidding toward some steep chasm that made her heady with anticipation. It felt like falling into nothing and everything all at once.

"I can't..." he gasped against her ear, but her head was buzzing, and his words were drowned, lost in the divine, slippery wet friction at the exquisite place their bodies were joined.

Her body heard his urgency, foresaw his imminent release, and responded to him as if the force of his cock into her flesh was a demand. She wrapped herself around him, digging her heels into the small of his back. She clung, tumbling with him into some abyss, as she felt him buck and shudder against her. Instead of plunging to what she felt might be her death, she did something unexpected. She soared, finding herself flowing, rising and rolling, lifted and awash with the whirling, drifting glide of flight, and she rode it out as if she had wings.

"Am I still dreaming?" she asked him as their breathing slowed. Their bodies were slick and slippery with a wetness that cooled them in the transition from passion to sleep.

He rolled to his side, his eyes lingering on her before conceding to her tug and letting her pull the covers up to her chin.

"Do you want to be dreaming?" His gaze was soft as he touched her bruised and battered lip and cheek with his finger.

"Maybe." She winced, remembering, grateful that for a few blissful moments she had forgotten. She pulled the covers over with her as she rolled away from him. He sighed as he slid behind her, his arm heavy across her ribs, but she didn't care. "I guess I'll know if I wake up here tomorrow, won't I?"

"Maybe." He fitted her hips against his.

She heard his breathing grow deep and even, cool against her cheek where her tears fell and then pooled at the hollow of her throat. She didn't even know why she was crying, but the tears kept coming even after she slipped toward sleep.

Chapter Ten

When she woke, it felt like Christmas morning. It wasn't, but she'd never felt so safe and warm and utterly calm. The bed was soft and inviting. The sound of Nick downstairs, banging pots and pans in the kitchen, made her smile. For a moment, it all disappeared. She didn't think about the past few weeks, the cold, the hunger, hiding and sleeping on the streets. She didn't think about Brody looking for her, about him catching her in the alleyway. She didn't think about the boys who had robbed the video store, who had clearly been watching, waiting for her to return so they could recoup their spoils.

In that moment, when she opened her eyes to the slant of morning light, none of that existed. She was just grateful to be breathing, alive, safe and warm. The night before had been one of the best and worst of her life. It was hard to reconcile that paradox, but as she stared up at the ceiling, she found herself thinking of Nick. Of his smile. His kindness. He'd been the one who left her peanut butter. The Scrunchie. He'd been watching, the whole time, but instead of stalking her, he'd been trying to make sure she was safe. Fed. Warm.

She got out of bed, finding her clothes folded on the dresser, washed and dried. Even her panties. A slow smile spread across her face, remembering the look in his eyes when she'd accidentally flung her panties out of her bag at him. She got dressed slowly—she was stiff and sore from the attack the night before—wondering how much Nick knew.

Ginny's backpack was sitting next to her clothes on the dresser. Her heart racing, she rifled through it, finding the little zipper pocket inside, where the SD memory card was hidden. There were three of them, but only one had the incriminating evidence on it. The other two were smaller and blank. She hadn't gotten to filling those for her project for the one community college class Brody had allowed her to take. She hadn't finished her project at all. Everyone else would be making their presentations before the semester ended for the holiday, but not her.

"Nick?" she called as she came down the stairs.

She found him flipping pancakes in the kitchen. The table was set, milk poured.

"Morning, angel." He smiled as she walked toward him, standing at the stove. "Hope you're hungry."

"Are you kidding me?" she scoffed. "When have you known me *not* to be hungry?"

"Good point." He smiled, sliding fluffy, golden pancakes onto a plate already filled with them. "I was going to come wake you with a kiss. Like sleeping beauty."

His gaze fell to her mouth and she smiled, putting her arms around his neck.

"Well, I'm not sleeping anymore, but I wouldn't say no to that kiss."

He kissed her, pancakes still in hand, his mouth soft, making her yearn for more.

"Thank you, Nick," she breathed, trying not to let her eyes fill with tears. "You've been... very good to me."

"I intend to keep on being very good to you." His eyes searched hers.

She took a seat at the table and waited for him to put pancakes on her plate before slathering them with butter and syrup. He watched her eat, looking thoughtful.

"Stop it," she finally said, taking a cold gulp of milk.

"Stop what?"

"Stop looking at me like that."

"Like what?" He gave her a quizzical smile, chewing a bite of pancakes.

"Like you're looking for some happy ever after I might have hidden up my sleeve." She pointed her fork at him. "You can't fix this."

"Ginny, you're wrong." He frowned. "I know you've had a bad experience with a cop…"

"A bad experience?" she choked, her eyes watering. "That's an understatement. The man was my stepfather, Nick."

"I know." His eyes darkened at the thought. "Ginny, I'm sorry. If I'd known…"

"No one knew." Her jaw tightened. "And no one is going to know. I'm leaving. And you can't stop me."

"Where are you going to go?"

"I can't tell you that." She shrugged.

"You said they took your bus ticket," he reminded her. Damn, the man had a memory like a steel trap. "Where was it to?"

"You swear…" She swallowed. "You swear you won't tell?"

"You want me to cross my heart and hope to die?"

"Maybe."

"Fine." He rolled his eyes, tracing his finger in an x-shape over his heart. "I swear. On my life. On this badge."

"California," she said finally. "I want to go to art school out there. I'm leaving the day after Christmas."

"Why did you wait?" He puzzled. "Why are you here? In town, I mean?"

"I didn't have the money for the ticket… before…" She didn't want to tell him about Maggie.

"Where did you get the money?"

"It kind of just… fell into my hands." She didn't want to tell him about the robbery either—about what she'd done with the money.

"So why after Christmas? If you're afraid Brody is going to find you, why didn't you hop on a bus right away?"

"It was cheaper if I bought it a week in advance," she told him. "I figured, I'd waited this long… what was a few more days?"

"He's not going to stop looking for you," he said softly.

"I know." She felt that with every breath. "But I have someone helping me. There's this network. A domestic violence shelter, sort of an underground railroad? I've been talking to a woman online. She's finding a family to take me in for a while, just until I get on my feet."

"You set that all up, on your own?" He looked at her, surprised.

She nodded.

"Ginny…" he said softly.

"Stop looking for a happily ever after, okay?" She frowned at him.

"I just want to do the right thing."

"Do you always do the right thing?" she asked.

"I try to," he replied. "That's what cops do, Gin. Most of us… we start out doing this because we just

- 109 -

want to help people. I mean, my dad's a cop, my grandfather was a cop…"

"I know." Of course, she knew. "Quite a legacy."

"I don't know if it's easier or harder, because of it." Nick shrugged. "My dad has always been a good cop. It's not easy living up to, when your dad's your boss."

She longed to tell him, but she knew she couldn't. How could she possibly?

"Well, Brody is definitely not a good cop."

"Obviously." He frowned. "Sometimes you just never know."

"Things aren't always what they seem." It was the closest she could come to telling him the truth.

"So, how are you going to make it to California now?" he asked quietly. He looked so sad at the thought, and her usual exhilaration about her plan had disappeared.

"Slowly." She sighed. "Before I bought the ticket, Kit—that's the woman online who's been helping me—said she found a family in Ohio who could take me in for a week or so. I was just going to go from house to house… until I made it out."

"You've been very brave, Ginny."

"I did what I had to do." She shrugged.

A knock on the door startled them both.

"Who is it?" she whispered, her face draining of color. She felt all the blood rush out of it.

"Probably just the mailman." Nick stood, heading toward the living room. "Stay here."

She did, frozen in place at the table. She heard voices, but it was a woman's voice, not a man's, and that filled her with relief. Not Nick's father, then. As long as she could get out there without him ever knowing she was there, it would be okay.

"Well, what are partners for? It's just not like you, Nick," the woman's voice came closer and Ginny stood, looking for the best place to hide. "I brought you some orange juice and some kale and some Echinacea. That should boost your immune system."

Ginny walked halfway into the broom closet when the woman burst into the room carrying a bag of groceries. She was a pretty woman, wearing a uniform, her dark hair pulled back tight, away from her face. She eyed Ginny, half in and half out of the closet, both of them blinking in surprise.

"I told you, I'm fine, Suzanne," Nick protested, coming in behind the woman, seeing Ginny standing there, eyes wide. "It's just a touch of... something..."

"I see that." Suzanne put the grocery bag down on the counter. "Who's this?"

"I'm cleaning the house." Ginny closed the door to the broom closet, broom in hand, and stood there, heart beating so fast in her chest she thought it might burst right there. "Just here to clean the house. I'll get started, Mr. Santos. In the... um... bathroom..."

She edged her way around Nick's partner, recognizing her now. She was the woman in the photographs on the mantle. Still sitting on the mantle. This woman, this Suzanne, was clearly Nick's partner—in more ways than one. A slow burn filled her chest, a growing feeling of jealousy, and she silently chastised herself. She didn't have any reason—or right—to be jealous.

"Thanks," Nick said, blinking in surprise as Ginny went past him.

Ginny saw Suzanne eyeing their dishes, half eaten pancakes still on their plates. At least I didn't come down wearing just his shirt, she thought, locking herself in the downstairs bathroom. She could hear them talking still, the voices but not the words. She sat on the closed toilet lid, sitting there trembling. She needed to get out of there, as fast as she could. Maybe she could contact Kit online, see if the family would take her before Christmas.

She would miss saying goodbye to Maggie and the boys, which broke her heart, but if she had to do it, she would. She'd find a way. She always did.

"Ginny?" Nick's voice, on the other side of the door. "Ginny, are you okay?"

"Is she gone?" Ginny asked, reaching a shaking hand out for the knob.

"She's gone."

Ginny opened the door, looking up at him, at the concerned look on his face.

"I'm sorry about that," he apologized, reaching out to take her hand. His swallowed hers. "I didn't think she would come by."

"She's…" Ginny swallowed. That jealous feeling was back. "She's the woman on your mantle. She's… your partner?"

"Just at work," he smiled, pulling her against him. She let him. She felt safe there, in his arms. "We're over, otherwise. She's got a new boyfriend. Suzanne's just… nosey."

"Typical cop." Ginny smirked, looking up at him, and he laughed.

"Come on, let's go finish breakfast before it's cold."

But it was already cold. Ginny helped him clean up the plates, loading them into the dishwasher. Neither of them talked much, but she could tell he was thinking—

about her, about Brody, about everything she'd told him. And she hadn't even told him the half of it.

"Hey." Nick took her into his arms, tilting her chin up so he could look at her. "Are you okay?"

"No." She gave him a half-hearted smile. "Haven't been okay in a long time. But I'm alive. That's something."

"I'm so sorry." He frowned, putting his arms around her. "I wish I could make it better for you."

"You can't," she whispered, shaking her head. It was the truth. No one could. There was no solution here. There was only one way out, and she had to take it. Soon.

"I can try." He kissed the top of her head. "We need to make sure you're safe, Ginny. And I don't mean for the moment. I mean forever."

"How do you propose to do that?" She glanced up, cocking her head at him, seeing the conflict there in his eyes. "Oh no. No, no, no. I'm not making any reports. I'm not talking to any more cops."

"Ginny…" He sighed as a phone went off in his pocket. He let her go to reach in and retrieve it and she watched as he checked the message. "Shit."

"What?" she frowned as he slipped his phone back into his pocket.

"They're calling me in." He made a face. "I've got to go."

"But you called in sick?"

"They want everyone." His brow knitted as he looked down at her. "Some sort of domestic disturbance. A hostage situation."

"A what?" She gaped at him, shocked. "In Lewisonville?"

"Christmas can bring out the worst in people." Nick took her by the upper arms, holding her out in front of him, his gaze serious, voice earnest. "Ginny, stay here. Please, just stay here. Don't go anywhere. Don't run off, okay? Will you promise me that?"

How could she possibly promise him that? She'd been looking for a way out, and here it was, like a Christmas miracle. She could slip away, get out of town, and he would never be able to find her again. No one would. So why did the thought make her feel so awful, so terribly sad?

"Ginny, please." He moved his hands up to cup her face, searching her eyes. "I just found you again. I don't want to lose you."

His words sent little knives into her heart. She felt her eyes getting wet.

"Okay," she breathed, trembling, going against her better judgment.

"You promise?" he urged.

"Yes," she whispered, tilting her face up when he kissed her, his mouth bringing back the warm memory of the night before, how her body had responded to him, completely surprising her. This man kept surprising her, again and again.

It only took him five minutes to get into uniform. He kissed her again at the front door like he thought he might never see her again, despite her promise.

"Don't answer the door," he insisted. "Lock it behind you. Don't answer the phone either."

She nodded in agreement.

"You can watch TV," he told her, and then grinned. "Eat whatever you want, my little piglet."

She laughed and made a grunting noise. That made him laugh, too, and hug her close, burying his face in her hair.

"We'll work this out," he murmured against her ear. "We'll work something out."

"Okay." She agreed, even if she didn't quite believe it.

"I'll be back as soon as I can," he assured her, that concerned look back in his eyes. "Just… stay put."

"I will, I will!" she agreed, laughing, waving him out the door.

She peeked out the window, saw him get into his car—a navy blue Impala, not his squad car—and watched him drive away, a sinking feeling in her belly. This was impossible. Just impossible. He said they would work it out, but how? There was no working this out, and she knew it.

She went upstairs, looking at the bed where they'd spent the night, the memory making her feel both warm and sad. He'd asked her to stay, and she would. For now. But she couldn't stay forever. She couldn't possibly do what he wanted her to do. Giving him that SD card would not only put her and her family in jeopardy—it would hurt him too. Maybe someday he would find out the kind of man his father really was, but she didn't want to be the one who revealed that to him. She didn't want him to know what they'd done to her. It was too awful, too humiliating.

Ginny decided to take a shower and maybe another little nap after that. When she got dressed again, it was just one layer of clothes for the first time in a long time, which felt so strange. She was used to being bundled up against the cold. She stopped to check her backpack again, sitting on the bed and pulling out her sketch book. She considered working on her drawings—the coloring books she was making for the boys were almost done—but she didn't feel quite up to it.

Her stomach was in knots. She decided to warm up some milk—that always made her feel sleepy. She left the pad on the night table, and on the way to the stairs, she passed Nick's bedroom, just glancing in on the way by. The view stunned her, and she found herself drawn to his window. She stood there until she could see her breath appearing on the glass.

It was still snowing heavily outside, a good foot of snow covering the ground, a truly magical sight, but that wasn't what astonished her now. From this vantage point, she could see into the video store lobby. She was staring at the corner she had slept in for weeks.

He'd known she was sleeping there. He was Mr. Peanut Butter. Mr. Scrunchie. She'd been so thrilled, at the time, to find them, thinking someone had just thrown them away, but the truth was, he'd left them for her. He'd been watching over her, the whole time.

And what, exactly, did he see?

Ginny swallowed, remembering how fast he'd been on the scene the night before.

But she hadn't been there in a week. She hadn't gone back to the video store on purpose, not after the robbery, too afraid they would be there, waiting.

Had he seen that, too? Did he know she'd taken the money?

The thought filled her with a cold sort of dread, a horrible shame. She had to tell him the truth. Oh God, she had to tell him all of it. If she wasn't going to leave—and she promised him she wouldn't, and meant it, at least for now—she was going to have to tell him. Everything.

That night last year around this time, the night Brody let his buddies take her, use her, had just been the first. The first of many. As guilty as she felt for taking the money, she was far more ashamed of how she'd let it all happen. That night under the Christmas tree last year had been awful, but she didn't leave. Maybe she'd expected it all along, after what had happened to Maggie.

She didn't fight Brody—she didn't fight any of them. She just floated away while it happened and cleaned up afterward like it hadn't. It was the last time—the time caught on tape, preserved on the SD memory card in her backpack—that had finally broken her. They had raped her, all three of them—Maggie's husband, Tim, included—in all that blood.

Ginny remembered cleaning up that night. There was blood all over—blood in her hair, on her face, everywhere. She'd washed it away, but this time, she couldn't wash away the feelings, like she usually did. Maybe it was Tim's face, her sister's own husband, poised above hers in a grim snarl, that finally did it. Maybe it was overhearing them talking about her, the way Brody laughed when the other cop, Steve, talked about getting rid of her, along with the body.

"She's not going to say anything," Brody insisted as Ginny stood at the top of the stairs, scrubbed clean and listening. "Trust me."

It felt like it had happened a million years, to some other girl.

She'd packed her bag in the middle of the night, had checked the video camera—they never even noticed it—and removed the SD card. In the morning, after Brody went to work, she'd left a note, telling him if he ever tried to find her, she would tell. That she had evidence, and it was damning.

Then she'd gone to Maggie's. Their house was just a mile away, and it would be the first place Brody would look, but she needed money. Tim's car wasn't there, and she took a chance, knocking on Maggie's door, only to find her sobbing. Their bank account was empty. Tim was gone. And Ginny knew why. The dead man, the rape. He'd skipped town because he wasn't a cop—but the other two were. They could easily pin a crime like that on a known addict.

But she couldn't tell her sister that.

She wouldn't have even known about the shelter if it wasn't for Mr. Spencer. He had told her about it, back in seventh grade, when Maggie had gotten pregnant. He'd pulled Ginny aside and told her there was a place in Lewisonville where Maggie could go— no one would know. They were anonymous, he said. Invisible. Even Brody didn't need to know, he'd told her with a knowing look.

He'd suspected, she thought, but he hadn't known.

Maggie didn't go, though. She didn't want to leave her little sister. Instead, she had given birth to her stepfather's baby, pretending it was Tim's. And Tim pretended too. Everyone pretended it was all okay. Even Ginny pretended, when Maggie moved out, and Brody started coming into her room at night, now that Maggie was gone, that it was all okay.

Except she was sick of pretending. She was sick of lying and hiding the truth. She wanted to tell someone, she wanted to, finally, once and for all.

Downstairs, the sound of the door filled her with both relief and dread.

"Nick?" she called, her voice shaking.

She would tell Nick the truth, the whole truth, and he would know what to do. Somehow, she believed him when he said they would work it out. She smiled through her tears, taking the stairs down two at a time, and for the first time in a long time, maybe in forever, she felt happy.

Chapter Eleven

Steven Santos was a big man, but he wasn't fast. Ginny would have escaped him, coming casually through the front door, using a key pulled from under the mat, if the damned back screen door hadn't stuck in the snow. There was a good foot out back and Nick hadn't shoveled his back porch. Nick's father caught her by the length of her still-wet hair, yanking her back from the door and slamming it closed.

"I don't think so, sweetheart," he snapped. Her feet scrambled on the tile, but she couldn't go anywhere. Her scalp burned where he had a fist full of her hair. "You've led us on a merry little goose chase, haven't you? And you were under my damned nose the whole time."

"Please," Ginny whispered, but she knew it was useless. "Nick will be home any time."

"No, he won't." The old cop chuckled, his teeth stained with tobacco as he flashed her a knowing smile. "I know, because I had dispatch call him in."

Of course, he had. Ginny's whole body was going cold. Already, she felt numb. Resigned.

"Where's the tape?" He jerked her head back, so she had to look into his eyes. His face was round, puffy, lines deep around his eyes.

"In my bag. Upstairs." Tears filled her eyes, but not from the pain in her mouth when his crushed her own, her bruised lips aching, but because she realized she wasn't ever going to see Nick or Maggie or the boys, ever again.

"Let's get it, slut." He pushed her, and she sprawled, face first, on the kitchen tile. The air went out of her lungs so fast and hard, she didn't even have enough left to gasp.

He had her by the hair again before she could take a breath, shoving her up the stairs. He knew the way, of course—it was his son's house. Ginny pointed to the guest room when Steve went to turn into Nick's.

"He didn't even fuck you?" The old cop chuckled. "Fucking pansy-ass bitch. Dudley goddamned Do-Right."

Ginny didn't say anything to this. She still couldn't speak. She just pointed to the backpack she'd left on the floor beside the bed. Her sketch book was still sitting there on the night stand where she'd left it.

"Get it, whore." He shoved her forward and she fell against the bed, hitting her chin on the edge of the night stand. She didn't even cry out, although it hurt like hell. It was just one more bruise. What did it matter now?

Ginny dug into her bag, wondering if he was going to shoot her, once he had the evidence. Would he kill her right here, in Nick's house? She didn't think so. He would take her somewhere, she realized. And Nick—Nick would believe she had just left. There was no breaking and entering, the man had used a key. No signs of a struggle. She would just be gone.

No! I promised him! Her fingers found the compartment in her backpack lining and she unzipped it. Even if she died today—and she had a horrible feeling she would—she couldn't let Nick believe she'd just left him. Her fingers brushed the SD memory cards—one big one, two small. She knew exactly which was which, and suddenly, she had an idea.

"Here," she croaked, pulling one of them out and showing him.

"Good girl." He gave her a slow smile, taking the card and slipping it into his front pocket. "That's a start."

A start? She stared up at him from the floor, filled with both hate and dread.

"You're going to have to be taught a lesson." He grabbed her again by the hair, bringing her head close to his crotch and grinding his erection against her cheek. She wanted to cry, to scream, to kick and bite him, but it was no use. Fighting would only make things worse, cause more pain.

That's what Maggie had said to her, when Ginny got up the nerve to ask her once, why she didn't fight Brody when he went into her room at night.

Fighting just makes it worse.

She was trapped, and she knew it.

"Come on, I'm not the only one looking forward to teaching you a lesson." The cop yanked her to her feet and she whimpered at the pain. Her head hurt already.

"Get your stuff," he instructed, nodding at her backpack. "Is that it?"

"Yes." She nodded miserably, reaching for her bag, but she was brought up short by the hand in her hair.

"Get it!" he growled, shoving her again.

She fell again, this time to her knees on the floor. The tears welled up and, even though she willed them away, they fell onto her shaking hands as she struggled with the zipper. She hoped her body hid the way her hand dipped back into that little compartment—still unzipped—

and took out the largest SD memory card. She hid it in her palm as she pulled the main zipper closed.

- 122 -

"Okay." She stood, wobbly, putting the backpack over her shoulder.

"You got a coat?" He scowled at the tears making their way down her cheeks.

"Downstairs." She adjusted the backpack straps, glancing over her shoulder, seeing her sketch book still sitting there. "Are we going somewhere?"

She knew where they were going—or at least, she had a good idea. But she wanted to distract him while she adjusted and pulled at her straps, reaching back as if she was moving the weight of the bag. The SD memory card in her palm was so tiny. Would Nick find it? She knew the only hope she had was to get it into her sketch book.

He would never believe she'd just left her sketch book behind.

"Come on." The cop grabbed her arm, but thankfully it was the other arm. She was holding the SD memory card in the other hand.

"Ow!" She complained, shaking her arm away from him, using the motion to slip the SD memory card in between the pages.

Please don't let it fall out. Please don't let Steve see it. Please let Nick find it. Please...

"Stupid bitch." He grabbed a pair of handcuffs off his belt, turning her around and slapping them on, first one wrist, then the other. "Get going."

More shoving. Down the stairs, toward the front door. Steve grabbed her coat and shoes—she pointed them out near the door. She was handcuffed and couldn't put them on. He kept her in front of him, her stocking feet freezing in the snow as they made their way to the squad car parked out front. Ginny glanced around, hoping, praying someone would see them, but she didn't see anyone. The snow was still falling, and everyone was tucked away inside, bracing for the storm Nick had said was coming.

Steve pushed her into the back of the squad car and Ginny toppled over. She had no balance at all, her hands behind her, the backpack heavy on her shoulders. The car took off down the street as she struggled to right herself. Maybe she would see someone she knew? Maybe they'd even run into Nick? But Steve took back roads, all the way to the highway, and once they were on their way, she knew her suspicions had been right.

He was taking her home.

Ginny had missed the target but hit the tree with her guess. They ended up in Millsberg, but he didn't take her home. The house he pulled into was on the edge of town, at the end of a dirt road, and by the time they got there, it was growing dark. There were no neighbors, not even any other houses Ginny could see, but Steve parked the cruiser out back anyway, behind the house.

Everything ached. She was really feeling it, the attack in the vestibule, the way Steve had manhandled her, and she knew it was just the beginning. The beginning of the end. She couldn't help thinking of Maggie and the boys as she stumbled out of the car, her stocking feet getting wet again in her walk up to the house.

And she thought of Nick.

She had a glimmer of hope that he might, he just might, discover her sketch pad. He just might open it up and find the SD card inside. But would he find it in time? She looked up at Brody's face, sneering at her from the back door as the other cop shoved her forward, and knew it wasn't likely. Whatever happened between now and then would break her, once and for all, one way or another.

"Welcome home, Ginny." Brody opened the door wide and she had no other choice.

"Are you fucking kidding me?" The voice was faint. Ginny lifted her aching head from the mattress where they'd left her. It smelled like alcohol, urine, and vomit. She didn't want to know what had happened on that mattress—and she didn't want to know what was going to happen on it.

She was already floating by the time they'd handcuffed her to the bedpost. Her backpack was gone. So were most of her clothes. At least she wasn't wearing wet socks anymore, she thought, shivering on the bed as Brody stripped her down to her t-shirt. She thought she knew what was coming, but it didn't happen. At least, not right away.

They handcuffed her and left her, cold, alone, shivering, to await her fate.

To think about things. About everything. She thought about Maggie and the boys. It was only a few more days until Christmas. She'd promised she'd be there on Christmas day. She wanted to see the boys' faces when they saw what Aunt Ginny had made for them, but she knew she wouldn't be. She thought about Nick. She'd been so wrong about him. He was the opposite of his father, of Brody, she realized. All along, he'd just been trying to help her.

Now it was too late for that.

She might have slept. She couldn't remember. Mostly, she floated. She was far away, flying through the spaces in between snowflakes. Her world was upside down and she was inside that strange snow globe, tumbling around in the darkness. There was no bottom here, but there was no anchor either. She was lost, to everyone and everything.

"Get her up!" It was Brody's voice.

Rough hands grabbed her. Her wrists were raw and aching from the cuffs and she rubbed them when Steve unlocked them both.

"Where is it?" Brody slapped her so hard it rocked her backwards onto the bed. Her face stung and her ears rang so loud she couldn't even hear him yelling at her.

She knew what he wanted, but she wasn't going to tell him. She didn't dare.

"What the hell are you doing?" Brody snapped.

Ginny only saw them all in shadow—the room was still dark—but there was a third man. She was almost sure of it. It wasn't Steve's beefy hands who put something around her neck. She didn't know what it was until it tightened, yanked hard, and she choked. It was a dog chain, she realized, as she was pulled from the bed.

"Teaching her a lesson!"

Tim.

She knew his voice. It was Maggie's husband.

"Please," she gagged, crawling on hands and knees as Tim yanked the chain, dragging her out of the darkened room. The tile was filthy, but she crawled forward, following him. Brody and Steve brought up the rear. She knew she shouldn't speak, shouldn't beg or plead.

It would only make things worse.

"Where is it, goddamnit?" Brody's boot landed squarely on her behind and Ginny found herself sprawled on the dirty tile at their feet. "Where's that fucking memory card, you little bitch?"

So, they did know. Ginny cried out when another boot landed in her ribs and she closed her eyes, praying now for an end. It would come, she knew, but not soon enough. Not nearly soon enough. *Float, float.* That's what she needed to do. She needed to fly away. Far away. And never come back.

The gunshot rang out over her head and she screamed, brought back from the comforting darkness. The chain around her neck tightened and she choked, seeing Brody's face as she rolled to her back. He was holding the end of the leash now.

"What the fuck?" Brody yelled. He was ducking down, near her, and she saw Steve standing over his shoulder, a frown on his fat face.

Ginny strained, looking around, trying to see what was happening. Tim had his gun drawn and it flashed in his hand. He was pointing it down a dark hallway.

"Let her go!"

Nick.

Oh my God, it was Nick! Ginny's heart soared and then sank. He could be killed. He *would* be killed. It was three against one. Oh, what had she done?

"Listen, son," Steve's voice rang out, calling down the darkened hall. "You don't want to do this now. It's just a misunderstanding."

"I don't think so." There was steel in Nick's voice. "I've called in both the state cops and internal affairs. We can do this stand-off until then, or you can let the girl go."

"Nick, listen to me!" Steve's voice rose as he called to his son. "This isn't what you think!"

"No?" The anger in Nick's voice was almost palpable. "Because I have a recording of you raping that girl, Dad, in a pool of blood. I'm pretty sure this is exactly what it looks like."

Ginny felt the chain around her neck tighten so much she could barely breathe. Brody had her up on her knees, her fingers digging into her own throat, trying to relieve the pressure.

"You better come out here, boy." Brody let the chain go slightly and Ginny gasped for breath. "Or I'm going to shoot this bitch in the fucking head. I have no problem with that."

"Nick!" she croaked. "Go! Just go!"

The chain tightened again, and she gagged, pulled hard against Brody's thigh. He had a gun in his hand and it was pointing, like Tim's, down that dark hall.

"Ginny, are you okay?" His voice was pained.

She couldn't answer him. The choker chain was tight again and she was seeing stars. She saw Steve creeping forward out of the corner of her eye.

"She's gonna be dead in a minute." Brody was smiling. She could hear it in his voice.

"You're going to jail, you motherfucker." Nick yelled down the hallway. "No matter what happens, you're going to fry!"

"Oh, I don't think so." Brody's gun was drawn and up. "Not me, boy. This is an easy fix. A drug deal gone bad."

Two shots rang out in succession and Ginny stared in horror as both Tim and Steve dropped to their knees on the dirty tile. Tim's face was a mask of shock as he fell backward, staring up at the ceiling with wide, dead eyes. *He shot him. He shot them both!*

Steve Santos fell sideways, not backwards. Ginny couldn't see his face, only the bloody mess of the man's head. Part of her was floating away. She could almost see herself, dressed in panties and a bra, choker chain around her own neck, at Brody's feet like some human pet. It would have been kind of comical, really, if it wasn't so awful. She was up on her knees like a dog begging for a bone.

She heard Nick cry out. Had he been shot too? Ginny felt herself go cold at the thought. She couldn't let anything happen to him. It would be all her fault if it did, and even if she died here tonight, living with that thought, even for a moment, was too painful to bear.

Ginny threw her head back with as much force as she could, letting out a scream she hoped everyone in a five-mile radius could hear. The back of her skull connected with Brody's crotch and he screamed too. It was the most beautiful sound she'd ever heard in her life, even if her head was exploding with stars.

"Nick! Nick!" Her voice was hoarse, but she got the words out as Brody went to his knees behind her, groaning. It gave him just enough time, just enough of an opportunity.

Nick acted so fast it was a blur. Ginny's vision was fading, the lack of oxygen to her brain finally catching up to her. She gasped on her hands and knees as the men wrestled, but when she glanced over, she saw it was Brody on the ground. Brody was the one on his back on the dirty kitchen floor, with a gun pointed at his head.

Then she heard the sirens. Nick really had called in backup.

"Sounds like the cavalry is here, Boy Scout." Brody gave him a slow, spreading smile.

"Yeah." Nick glanced over at Ginny. She was on her side on the floor, two dead men behind her. Her throat hurt, and it was hard to breathe. Things were fading in and out. "But it's too late for you."

She saw the flash of Nick's gun before she was gone, floating again between the stars.

"It's over, Ginny. It's all over." It was Nick's voice, his arms around her, that brought her back. She looked up at him in wonder, disbelief.

"I'm sorry," she whispered. Her voice was really gone now. "I promised I wouldn't leave…"

"You're not going anywhere else without me." Nick kissed the tears on her cheeks. She hadn't even known she was crying. "Not ever again. You hear me?"

She couldn't do anything but give him a faint, fading smile and a nod.

That was perfectly okay with her.

Epilogue

"Merry Christmas."

She felt a delicious shiver run through her at the sound of Nick's voice, his breath in her ear. She opened her eyes in a slant of morning light, squinting, stretching and yawning. She turned and saw he was lying next to her.

"Merry Christmas," she murmured—her voice was back—sitting up. The covers fell to her waist and she pulled them back up, giving him a little smile.

"I think Santa was here." He was admiring the curve of her hip, she noticed. "But let's get some breakfast first."

"What time is it?"

"About ten," he said. "Eggs, pancakes, bacon, sausage?"

"Yes," she replied without hesitation, and he laughed. "It's really ten?"

She found the shirt she'd been wearing the night before and pulled it over her head.

"Do you have somewhere to go?"

She stood, heading toward the door. "Actually, yes."

He raised his eyebrows at her, but she just smiled and shut the bathroom door, starting the shower. Once she was clean and dressed she looked at her face in the mirror. Her wounds had healed somewhat, her face no longer full black and blue. The bruises had faded to a streaky sort of sunset.

She made her way downstairs and found Nick in the living room in front of the lit fireplace, drinking coffee and staring at the Christmas tree.

"Pretty," she remarked. It was a real tree. She loved the fresh pine scent as she passed and sat down opposite him on the couch.

"Yes," he replied, looking at her and not at the tree. "Do you want to see what Santa left you?"

He smiled over the rim of his cup at her.

"Santa hasn't left me gifts since I was six." She laughed, and it was a bitter sound. "But I really would love breakfast."

Her rarely appeased stomach was growling quietly.

"Come on, go look."

"So, I guess you've been busy," she mumbled. "I didn't get you anything, you know. Didn't exactly know you were going to play knight errant to my damsel in distress."

"Fat man. Red suit. Ho-ho-ho." He grinned. "No worries. Just go ahead and look."

"Nick..." she started, frowning.

"Just look," he gently urged.

He encouraged her to retrieve her gifts from under the tree. She was like a fastidious child on Christmas morning, easing open the wrapped edges, folding the bright paper into careful squares. She relished every moment. He had bought her a drawing set, a book, pencils, several drawing pads, erasers, sharpeners, even a triangle and a blending stump. It was perfect.

"Thank you!" She leapt into his lap, straddling his long, thick thigh, and hugging him tight, feathering kisses over his cheek.

"Told ya. Santa left it." He captured her lips with his. Her bruised mouth was still sore, and she winced but managed to kiss him back.

"I've been waiting to do that for hours," he whispered into her hair. "Your little mouth finally relaxes when you're sleeping, did you know that? You look like an angel. Now, are you ready for breakfast?"

She didn't respond, she couldn't. Instead, she nodded, her arms going around him. She didn't know if she could take any more kindness. There was a thick lump in her throat that she was trying to swallow. She followed him to the kitchen, finding exactly what he had offered on her plate—bacon, sausage, eggs, and pancakes.

"You saw me, didn't you?" she asked after he had retrieved ketchup for her eggs. Less than a week of eating real food in a real kitchen and she was rediscovering a thing called preference. "You knew I was sleeping at the video store?"

They hadn't talked about it, not yet. They'd talked past each other about it. Nick had answered everything he needed to, telling the police how he'd found the memory card, had tracked his father's squad car to Brody's hunting property. There'd been lots of questions, from police officers in both towns, from doctors and nurses, but Nick hadn't asked her directly about it. Not once. It was almost as if he thought, by asking, she might disappear. She'd talked to Maggie—her sister knew what had happened, but Ginny hadn't let her come see her. She was afraid the boys would get too scared if they saw the bruises on her face.

"Well, I knew you were homeless, probably a runaway," he explained logically, pouring syrup. "I knew you needed help. I also knew if I approached you too fast, you'd just run again, and I didn't see how that was helping you."

She listened, chewing thoughtfully.

"But when I saw you rummaging through the garbage for food... God, Ginny, I couldn't stand it. So, I started leaving you things."

She nodded. "The Scrunchie?"

"Your hair is in your face all the time." He smiled, looking sheepish.

They ate in silence for a while and Ginny sipped her orange juice like it was liquid sunshine.

"What I don't understand..." he said, his voice changing a little bit as he mopped at his eggs with a piece of toast, "is what you did with the money?"

Her heart lurched in her chest and she covered it with her hand, sure it was going to leap out. Her face burned.

"You saw that too?" she whispered, although he had been clear, unmistakably clear. The look on his face was still pained, torn.

"I saw it all happen."

The silence roared between them. Ginny thought she had forgotten how to breathe for a moment.

"When you didn't come back, I thought you must have used the money to skip town. I was as surprised as I've ever been when I saw you there that night. I sat here, knowing I could make one phone call and do the 'right' thing..." He sighed, rubbing his fingers over his eyes. "I don't know what the right thing is anymore."

She didn't know what to say. Despite the delicious meal she had just eaten, she had an awful taste in her mouth.

"I didn't want it," she confessed. "I didn't know what to do with it. If I returned it, I was afraid I'd get caught. If I kept it, I was a thief."

"Yeah." He nodded.

"Do you really want to know where it went?" she asked him, her heart aching wide open.

"I don't know... Do I?"

She reached across the table and squeezed his hand. "Will you take me somewhere?"

"As long as it isn't a bus station," he said, his heart in his eyes.

She shook her head and smiled.

"Oh my God, your face! Is this Nick?" Maggie stood at the door in her nightgown, although it was almost noon, the boys chasing each other around inside the apartment behind her.

"Merry Christmas to you, too." Ginny smiled. "Can we come in?"

Maggie frowned, then hugged her, pulling her into the apartment, away from Nick. He stood in the hallway, hesitating, waiting.

"Come on." Ginny reached her hand out for him.

Maggie did her wide-eyed "What is this?" look behind Nick's back.

Ginny called to the boys. "Hey, guys, I'd like you to meet my friend, Nick."

A chorus of two screaming, "Aunt Ginny!" surrounded them in an instant. Ginny swept them both up, groaning under the weight.

"You guys need to stop getting so big. Sean, Michael, this is Nick." She made brief introductions, because they were already asking their mother if they could now open their presents from Aunt Ginny.

"Let them." Ginny smiled, pulling Nick over to the couch to sit.

The boys opened their respective packages with the same attitude they did everything, Sean tearing in without a second thought, Michael carefully lifting each taped edge.

"X-Men!" Sean exclaimed, flipping through the pages.

Maggie stared over his shoulder. "Oh my God, Ginny. Did you draw these?"

Ginny nodded, watching Michael's face as he goggled at Sean's book, and noticed he was edging his package open much faster now.

"You did?" Nick looked stunned. "Hey, buddy, can I see that?" he asked Sean, who reluctantly handed it over.

"I got Spiderman!" Michael exclaimed, delighted.

Nick glanced over at Michael's booklet of drawings, too, shaking his head in wonder. "Man, these are really good," he told her, leafing through them.

"That's my sister, the artist." Maggie smiled. "I keep telling her she needs to do something more practical, but she loves drawing so much..."

Maggie looked fondly at her anyway, and Ginny smiled back at her sister. Sean snatched his book back from Nick, going to compare his with his brother's.

Nick turned to Ginny, his eyes softening.

"When did you move?" he asked Maggie, not taking his eyes off Ginny's.

"It was such a gift, about a week ago, just in time for Christmas," Maggie told him, gathering up the wrapping paper on the floor. "We didn't have anything, we were living in a women's shelter..."

Nick nodded, his gaze moving over Ginny's face.

"We still don't have very much, just what was donated to us. At least the boys are getting a real Christmas, in a real home..." Her voice trailed off as she looked affectionately at her sons huddled together on the floor. She still hadn't told them about Tim, Ginny knew, and she didn't think she would, not right away.

There were some secrets worth keeping, she thought. She knew there were things she'd never share with her sister about what had happened. Nick knew. That was enough.

Ginny flushed when Nick lifted her chin and kissed her fully on the mouth. Both boys noticed and whooped. Maggie stood there with wrapping paper in her hands, stunned.

"Did I do the right thing?" Her voice trembled.

"You *are* the right thing," he whispered in her ear, and she felt something loosen in her chest, spreading like warm liquid through her middle.

They spent several hours with Maggie and the boys, Nick making numerous piggyback runs from their beds to the couch and back while Maggie listened across the kitchen table with growing horror to her sister's quiet tale. She hugged both Nick and Ginny tearfully as they left.

It was midafternoon when they got back to Nick's house. Ginny sat on the floor in front of the tree, looking into the fireplace. He settled himself behind her, pulling her close, and she snuggled back between his legs.

"Hey, you never looked in your stocking," Nick murmured, kissing her temple.

She tilted her head at him and then looked at the mantle. Yesterday, there was only one stocking there. Today, there were two.

"The red one," he prompted.

Her heart was beating fast, but she retrieved it and sat back down beside him. It felt empty. Wouldn't that just be too funny?

"What is this?" She reached into the bottom, all the way to the toe, and pulled out something very small. "Nick…"

"Open it."

Ginny flipped open the lid, revealing a beautiful platinum ring. She couldn't breathe.

"It was my mother's." He smiled when he said that. "I'll buy you something else if you want, but I thought…"

"It's beautiful. It's… really?" She blinked at him, too shocked to say anything else.

"Well, I told you I didn't want you going anywhere else without me." He put his arms around her waist. "Ever again, remember?"

"I remember." She stared at the ring in disbelief.

"You don't have to say anything now." His eyes searched hers. "I know it's too soon. I know it's actually kind of crazy. But I also know I love you, Ginny. I know it better than I know anything else."

She felt a lump growing in her throat. "I love you too, Nick."

"You do?" He brightened at this news, as if he'd actually wondered.

She searched his eyes for the truth and found it, searched her heart for her own, and found that as well.

She knew there was nothing she wanted more than to be here in this man's arms, feeling safe, protected, and for the first time in her life, truly loved.

"Yes," she whispered. "More than anything. Yes."

"That's a yes?" he asked, sounding uncertain.

"If you're proposing, I'm saying yes!"

"I'm definitely proposing!"

She flung her arms around him and kissed him hard, and the ring went flying.

"Shit!" Ginny swore, and they spent half an hour looking for it.

Finally, Nick found it tucked down into the recesses of the sofa and slipped it onto her finger. It was a little too big, so she put it on a different finger instead, too afraid to lose it until they could get it resized.

"Let's start this day over again," she said, tucking her head under his chin.

"Too much drama?" He smiled, teasing her.

"No," she assured him, snuggling against him in the light of the fire. "I just want to feel like this, with you, forever. I bet we've got a whole lifetime of drama left to live."

"I hope so," he whispered against the softness of her mouth.

They found each other again and again that night while the snow fell heavily, and the wind wailed outside, and Ginny finally discovered what a real home really felt like in his arms.

The End

GET SIX FREE READS

Selena loves hearing from readers!
website: selenakitt.com
facebook: facebook.com/selenakittfanpage
twitter: twitter.com/selenakitt @selenakitt
blog: http://selenakitt.com/blog

Get ALL SIX of Selena Kitt's FREE READS
by joining her mailing list!

ABOUT SELENA KITT

Selena Kitt is a NEW YORK TIMES bestselling and award-winning author of erotic and romance fiction. She is one of the highest selling erotic writers in the business with over two million books sold!

Her writing embodies everything from the spicy to the scandalous, but watch out-this kitty also has sharp claws and her stories often include intriguing edges and twists that take readers to new, thought-provoking depths.

When she's not pawing away at her keyboard, Selena runs an innovative publishing company (excessica.com) and bookstore (excitica.com), as well as two erotica and erotic romance promotion companies (excitesteam.com and excitespice.com) and she now runs the Erotica Readers and Writers Association.

Her books EcoErotica (2009), The Real Mother Goose (2010) and Heidi and the Kaiser (2011) were all Epic Award Finalists. Her only gay male romance, Second Chance, won the Epic Award in Erotica in 2011. Her story, Connections, was one of the runners-up for the 2006 Rauxa Prize, given annually to an erotic short story of "exceptional literary quality."

Her book, Babysitting the Baumgartners, is now an adult film by Adam & Eve, starring Mick Blue, Anikka Albrite, Sara Luvv and A.J. Applegate.

She can be reached on her website at:
www.selenakitt.com

YOU'VE REACHED

"THE END!"

Made in the USA
Las Vegas, NV
31 October 2023

80046710R00090